THE
NIGHT
HUNTERS

A BLACK BAT MYSTERY

THE NIGHT HUNTERS

BY

JOHN MILES

The Bobbs-Merrill Company, Inc.

INDIANAPOLIS / NEW YORK

The Bobbs-Merrill Company, Inc.
Indianapolis / New York

Copyright © 1973 by John Miles
ISBN 0-672-51810-4
Library of Congress catalog card number 72-89689
Printed in the United States of America
BOOK DESIGNED BY VINCENT TORRE

PROLOGUE

In the summer of 1962, the President of the United States flew 2,000 miles in order to cut a ribbon and open twelve miles of two-lane asphalt highway. The new road followed the ridged crest of a wooded hill system—steps to the Ozarks—in the most desolate and beautiful section of southeastern Oklahoma.

The President's aides spoke of his abiding interest in projects designed to preserve natural beauty and stimulate pride in the nation, and the President himself, standing tall and young with the brisk Oklahoma wind in his sandy hair, spoke movingly of our heritage.

It was not by any means an entirely cynical performance, but the President was a pragmatic man and he needed this trip for political reasons. John F. Kennedy had lost Oklahoma in 1960, was the target for mounting extremist hatred throughout the South and Southwest and needed exposure of this kind if he was to mend his fences. He thought he would run for the Presidency again in 1964 and was starting early.

Oklahoma's senior Senator, Robert S. Kerr, was also on hand for the ribbon-cutting, and he too stood to gain. His "land, wood and water" theme was paying off handsomely for his constituency in the Arkansas River Navigation Project, destined to open Oklahoma to the sea. But he was under fire for the project in some quarters, and he had helped engineer the President's trip here to demonstrate his own political muscle.

And so they stood on the little flag-festooned platform under the high blue Oklahoma sky, the young President who needed exposure to win friends and the aging Senator who needed the pros to see his clout, and both spoke movingly of the nation's natural beauty and heritage and of pride. Both men happened to believe in what they were saying, so they took pleasure in the things they said and said them truly. Because they were also both consummately professional politicians, they also took pleasure in having found this event where they could speak truly of something they believed, win friends and score strategic practical gains, all at the same time. This ability to meld theory with practicality, they both realized, was the thing that separated the statesmen from the dog catchers.

Senator Robert S. Kerr was five months away from a fatal heart attack.

The President was sixteen months away from Dallas.

But no one could predict this, and it was a jubilant day. The speeches were made, the ribbon was cut, the cars streaked onto the little road for a brief yet breathtaking ride along the ridge-line, and then it was over and the helicopters came and everyone went away and the tattered crepe streamers fluttered in the evening wind and it was quiet again and peaceful.

It was by all odds the biggest day in the history of the town of Noble in Archer County, Oklahoma. But even the biggest days fade quickly, and Noble looked like any other shabby little southeastern Oklahoma town that day in 1966 when Larry Concannon drove in.

A heavy man with a burr haircut and old tattoos purple and red on both forearms, Concannon visited Noble alone. He parked his aging Ford sedan at the Cherokee Motel, registered for the night and began asking questions about his old friend Spandecker.

"Spandecker?" the woman behind the motel desk repeated. She was about fifty, heavy, sloppy, gray. She frowned. "There's no one by that name in Noble. Never has been."

"That can't be," Concannon grunted. "Jerry Spandecker and me, we went all through Europe together in the war. He always talked about this town. He always lived here. He came back here. I had mail from him."

"There's a Noble in Cleveland County," the woman pointed out. "Maybe you're mixed up."

"No," Concannon insisted, puzzled.

The woman said Concannon might ask at the drugstore. She said Alvin Crewser, the druggist, knew everyone in the county. She gave Concannon directions.

Crewser shook his head and said the name was totally unfamiliar.

Flummoxed, Concannon stood on the sidewalk in front of the drugstore and tried to figure out what was going on. Noble was an old town, and the main street twisted back upon itself, ducking around a huge old redstone city building. Half the stores along the street were closed, boarded up. The occasional car going along the street rattled as its tires thudded into edges of broken pavement. It was clear that Noble had known better days. Some of the buildings were three stories tall, with ornate brickwork, castled windows, Victorian spires and turrets. Great old willows, sweetgums, elms and maples lined the twisted streets, giving them a soft shadow of elegant decay in the dying afternoon heat. There seemed to be no children.

Standing there, Concannon felt a chill. He wondered why.

But then, being a man not given to superstition, he stubbornly turned his mind back to his problem. He had driven more than six hundred miles to see his old friend and he intended to find him. Noble might be a decaying town, one that somehow gave him the shudders, and he could well understand if Jerry Spandecker had finally chosen to leave it for someplace more in the mainstream. But Jerry *had* been here; of this Concannon was certain. He was not losing his mind. The job was to find out where Jerry Spandecker had gone.

Concannon walked to the post office. He talked to the man behind the counter, who was not helpful. He said the post office did not give out information on former residents. Did that mean Spandecker *had been* a resident here? He hadn't said that, the man behind the counter replied.

By this time it was getting dark. Shadows lay deep across the streets, making the buildings look like prehistoric things crouched as if to spring in the night. The only sign of life on the entire street was the blinking red of a Coors sign at a corner tavern where three pickups were parked. Concannon went in, had a sandwich, asked his questions, got the same negative replies.

He drove back to the motel. He had been on the road since dawn, but, being a truck driver, he was in good shape for that kind of effort and was not ready for sleep. The puzzle gnawed at him. On impulse he picked up the telephone book, little more than a pamphlet, and riffled the pages to the name he sought.

And there, tingling, he saw it: *Spandecker, T., 336 Elm, 235-4476.*

Hardly able to believe it, he read the line several times. The initial was wrong, but the last name was unmistakable. Yet everyone had said there was no Spandecker in the area. *Why?*

To hell with it. Concannon picked up the telephone on the table and waited for the office to answer.

"Yes, sir?" It was the woman's voice.

Concannon gave her the number.

There was a pause, and then he heard her dialing it.

The telephone rang a very long time. There was no answer.

Concannon hung up and thought about it. He had the feeling he was into something very strange. But he thought, too, that it was just one of those mixups that he and Jerry would laugh about later tonight over a beer. Jerry had always been hell with the women, Concannon recalled; probably he had some wife trouble or something like that—had to be awfully careful. People had said that southeastern Oklahoma was a very remote part of the country, more clannish and secretive than most areas of the deep South which had that reputation. The people here didn't trust strangers, didn't like them. They were protecting Jerry, somehow. Jerry would laugh about it once they got together, and it would make some kind of story to tell them back in Kansas City next week.

After waiting awhile, Concannon tried the number again and again got no answer.

It was almost ten o'clock now. He was restless. He walked to the front office, where the fat woman sat in a peeling plastic armchair, watching the late news. She heaved herself to her feet when Concannon entered.

"Can you tell me how to get to Elm Street?" he asked.

She blinked. "Elm?"

"Elm," Concannon repeated. "It's in the telephone book." He half expected her to say there was no Elm.

"If you'll drive about five blocks south," she told him, "and then turn west, you'll run into it the second street over."

"Thanks." He started for the door.

"Are you visiting someone?" she asked.

Concannon turned and saw clearly the fear in her eyes. The woman was terrified. He caught the rank, primitive odor of her fear, and it was a thing he had never experienced before.

"Yes," he said abruptly and went out.

Driving the unfamiliar, deserted streets, he again tried to penetrate what might be going on here. It was as if he had gone through some invisible wall and had emerged in another dimension. The assurances that there was no Spandecker, the telephone that didn't answer, the shocking, feral terror in the woman just now, the black streets cloaked beneath great old trees—they were all alien to Concannon and almost frightening. He realized how alone he was here.

But then his practical side reasserted itself and he chuckled at his own timidity. It was all going to be a good laugh once he located Jerry or the relative whose name was listed for 336 Elm.

He drove to the address.

It was a narrow street, curved, no streetlights, with the huge old trees black overhead, forming an ebony tunnel. The houses, well back, were two-story, old, with great old roofs and gables, and pillars along front porches. In some of the houses, through shrubbery, Concannon could see feeble lights.

He got out where he thought 336 ought to be and walked along the broken sidewalk with weeds brushing his calves. He bent to peer closely at the rural-type mailbox beside the front gate and barely made out the proper number. The house appeared dark, but he decided to try. If there was indeed no answer, he would leave a note in the screen door.

He walked up the front steps, catching the distant odors of

rotting vegetation, wildflowers, tar and dust. Except for the racket of night insects in the trees overhead, it was deathly quiet. The house loomed gray and tall, square pillars supporting the heavy porch roof, windows black. As he walked closer, picking his way on the broken-slab walk, Concannon became aware of the clammy discomfort of his armpits and a dry, coppery feeling on his tongue. He told himself he was acting like a kid, spooked by the first shadow.

Then the shadows moved.

Startled, Concannon cried out involuntarily.

Then something crashed with unbelievable force into the side of his skull and he was down on the pebbled, rot-smelling pavement, and he was bleeding, and he felt the wire go around his neck. The wire sang tight, slicing into his flesh just above his Adam's apple, and it hurt—it was *killing* him, it hurt so, and his legs were thrashing; he clawed the air and the pavement with fingernails, he rolled and kicked and tried to tear the wire away, but it was all pain now and he had no breath; the hot needles of strangulation filled his lungs. He fought, trying to scream, trying to get free. It hurt so much, yet it was more distant now, and he thought, *They're killing me.* And then far back inside himself there was a long, long tunnel, black, with a little flame of guttering candle far down there at the end, and there was a convulsion, softly, and the flame went out.

CHAPTER 1

It was frighteningly hot.

Expertly steering her new Vega around the worst chuckholes in the ancient pavement, Ruth Baxter tossed her cigarette out and rolled the window up again quickly, anxious to let the air conditioning remove the blast of incredible heat she had let in. She had deluded herself that it might be cooler here near the Ozarks, and on the last leg of today's drive from Rolla, Missouri, she had been even hopeful. But the record heat wave engulfing the Southwest was not alleviated by the high pines and hills of southeastern Oklahoma; if anything, it seemed even more oppressive here in the odd little town that was her temporary destination, Noble.

Waiting impatiently at the traffic signal for the battered green pickup ahead of her to move, Ruth glanced at the panel clock and saw it was just three o'clock. Her plans were working out as they usually did. She still had time to ask some questions today, do some work at the library tonight—if there was one here—and finish up by noon tomorrow. She had done enough poking around for Uncle Carl on other trips to know exactly the kind of information she needed and where she was likely to find it.

With luck, then, Dallas and the Furniture Mart late tomorrow afternoon.

The pickup ahead of her finally moved, turning right onto what was the main street, and Ruth followed. The outskirts of the town had been old, tree-shaded, decaying; a once nice community gone past gentility into depressing old age of the kind that allows sheds to sprout on weedy lots, great old houses to stand in ruins, gas stations to stare vacantly on corners behind crumbled pavement and abandoned pumps. So she was not too surprised by the tiny downtown section, which she now viewed.

It was about two and a half blocks long, and it bent sharply to the left at the far end. On her right were old brick buildings, some one-story and some two, several of them closed, with old circus posters plastered over boarded windows. On her left in this block were a small appliance store, its blue glass front in garish contrast to the yellow brick façade of the domino parlor next door, and then the ornate face of the old post office, a Chevrolet dealer's showroom with no cars on the floor and an ancient Esso station on the corner with several pickups parked in front of the littered garage area. The next block was more of the same—a drugstore, a closed theater, a small grocery, a variety store with plastic lawn chairs stacked out front, other little businesses, a café with a beer sign in the window.

The buildings at the far end of the street, where it curved, caught Ruth's eye. One was a huge, fading white grain elevator that appeared deserted. Next to it in irrational juxtaposition was a tall (four-story?), ornate redstone building, three rugged old turrets along the front, tall casement windows, a cathedral-type doorway, a flagpole in front on the tiny lawn, room air conditioners jutting irreverently from several of the front windows. Official parking signs lined the curb in front.

The city building, Ruth decided. Noble was not the county seat of Archer County; the handbook had told her that. But there would be some old records in this hall somewhere, and they were what she was after right now. A trip to the county courthouse in Puntman probably wouldn't even be necessary.

Looking for a place to start, she decided on the drugstore, with its red sign out front proclaiming CREWSER's. She pulled in to the curb, angle-parking next to a battered old Pontiac.

An old man, strolling along past the store, paused to stare for an instant at her New York license plate.

2

Ruth set the parking brake, turned off the ignition and quickly stepped out of the car into the breathtaking heat. The old man who had been staring at the plate now stared at her a moment before shuffling on. Probably the visitors from New York were few and far between. And a lavender pants suit probably was not Noble's community standard for women.

Amused, Ruth walked to the drugstore entrance and stepped inside. Welcome cold air enveloped her.

It was the kind of drugstore she hadn't seen for a long time. Big paddle fans extended from the high metalized ceiling. There were racks of merchandise everywhere in no apparent order, and behind the glass counters to the right were shelved myriad boxes of old tonics, cough medicines and medicating soaps she hadn't known were still in existence. Down a narrow aisle to the left was a soda fountain, complete with stools that had looped wire legs and backs. In an Eastern antique shop those stools would have brought a fortune.

A pretty, slightly plump girl of late high-school age stood behind the counter to the right. She smiled at Ruth. "Can I he'p you?"

Ruth went over. "A pack of Winstons, please."

The girl got the pack off the shelf behind her. "There you go," she said brightly. "Forty-two."

Ruth paid for the unneeded pack of cigarettes and put them in her purse. "It's hot out there," she observed tentatively.

"Golly, yes! You on a trip? You sure picked a hot day to be driving!"

"I'm going to be staying here the rest of the day and probably tonight. Is there a motel?"

"Gee, yes. You must have come in on the new road, the one that comes from the turnpike. If you go back out this way two blocks and then turn left, where you came in straight at the stop sign, you'll come to the Cherokee Motel. It's real nice."

"Good. I—"

"Where are you going?"

"Dallas."

"Gee! I got to go to Dallas last summer. It's a real nice place!

But you're not from Dallas. I mean, I saw your license plates and they're from New York."

They didn't miss much. But the girl's open curiosity was refreshing. This was quite a different kind of country. Ruth had to remember that.

"Actually," she told the girl, "I do live in New York. I'm going to Dallas on business. I stopped by here because I'm looking for some information. Possibly you can help me."

"New York! Golly, I've never been in New York, but I've got a girl friend whose mama and daddy went there last year. Information? I'll sure he'p you any way I can."

"I doubt that you can tell me what I want to know, but maybe you can direct me. A man named John Bartelson came here many years ago. About 1911. He had a clothing store here for a while. He went to the Army in the First World War. He came back afterward. We know he's dead now, but we don't know anything else. I want to find out all I can about him."

The girl made a face. "Bartelson? Bartelson? Gee, I never heard of anybody by that name. How come you need to know about him?"

"My uncle is a genealogist," Ruth explained; then, seeing the blank expression, she added, "He collects information about the family tree. John Bartelson was his mother's brother."

"Gosh, that's exciting! And you told your uncle you'd stop here on your way to Dallas and try to find out stuff for him!"

"That's right. I imagine—"

"Gee, I never *heard* of Bartelson! But you just wait a minute. I bet if anyone in this town would know, Mr. Crewser would. He's been here a long time and he knows just about *everybody*."

Ruth started to ask if Crewser was in the store, but the girl had already turned and flipped down the counter toward the back, calling, "Mr. Crewser? There's a lady here . . ."

Ruth lit a cigarette.

The man who came up from the labyrinth at the back of the store was just a little surprising. Ruth had been ready for a portly, fuddling little man, but Crewser was quite tall, gray-haired, dis-

4

tinguished. His slightly prominent nose was thin, like the rest of him, and gave his face strength. He wore a nice, if old, summer suit and tie.

He smiled warmly. "I'm Alvin Crewser. Sharon tells me you have a problem."

"Not a problem, really," Ruth said.

"Ancestor hunting?"

"For an uncle who's very dear and a little silly. The name I'm looking for is John Bartelson."

"I remember him."

"You do? Good."

"It was a long time ago. You're right about his dying way back. It must have been . . . let's see. I know I was in high school, so it must have been about '34, '35, along in there. He had a general store for a while just down the block. My father had this place then." Crewser paused and shook his head. "John Bartelson. I haven't thought about him for years."

"Did he have any family?"

"No. None at all."

"He died in about 1934?"

"Around there, yes."

"Do you have any idea if he had any good friends who might still be living?"

Crewser's smile held. His eyes watched her sharply, with keen, warm interest. "That generation is just about gone."

"I recognize that," Ruth replied, irritated.

"He was always sort of a loner, too. A nice man, as I recall him. I suppose I knew him as well as anyone still around here. But he kept to himself. I doubt very seriously if you'll find anyone who can give you much information."

"I think I probably can."

"Good at this, are you?"

"Efficient," she told him.

"I guess you are." His smile offered friendship.

"Thank you for your help," she said crisply, starting to turn away.

"Of course you could get his death date off his gravestone," Crewser volunteered. "I remember there being a little marker of some kind. The cemetery isn't far out of town."

"Yes," Ruth said. "Thank you again. Do you have a library?"

"In the city building. Not a bad library. Small, but we have old newspapers, standard references—"

"I'll look through those. And the city records."

"No need to do that," Crewser told her with the same intent smile. "He was such a quiet person, I feel sure you'd be wasting your time."

"That's my problem, then, Mr. Crewser. Is that the city building just down the block?"

"Yes. But I really do hate to see you waste your time. I'll tell you what I could do. I could go out to the cemetery with you. I think we could find his marker easily enough. That would give you what you need to know, wouldn't it?"

Ruth was patient. He might just want to be nice. "I think I'll check the records first and then possibly go to the cemetery on my way out of town tomorrow."

"You plan to stay overnight?"

"Is that really your concern?"

Crewser grinned and shook his head. "I'm afraid it's going to be an awful waste of time. If I were you, I'd just check that cemetery. I'm sure there just isn't any other information."

"We'll see," she said briskly.

"You don't like getting advice, do you?"

"It's not that I'm ungrateful. But I have my own ideas. And I do have some experience in this."

Crewser nodded, and his smile suddenly seemed forced. "Suit yourself. Be a waste of time, I'm afraid."

"Genealogists don't waste time, Mr. Crewser. They just narrow down possibilities."

Outside, the heat seemed even more intense. It smothered her, wrapped itself around her and pressed in everywhere, making breathing difficult. She considered driving the half block to the great old castlelike building but remembered the no-parking signs everywhere and decided to walk. She paused at the car long

6

enough to get the little briefcase of charts and notepaper out of the trunk. Then she walked along the empty sidewalk. The stillness was unreal.

It was almost an adventure, she thought. Passing a boarded-up store with trash and old newspapers cluttered in the V-shaped entryway, she realized she had never been in a place quite like this. In New York it was always the clamor of rebuilding or the despair of the ghetto, but in either case the experience teemed with life. Here there was not that kind of life. Here, behind the old store fronts, were only silence, emptiness, memory.

Passing a little, narrow barbershop, with the lone barber perched in his old-fashioned chair watching her over a magazine, she felt a chill. She told herself she was being awfully silly. A woman who took care of herself in New York could take care of herself practically anywhere. And wasn't she proud of her self-reliance?

The city-building steps were tall and steep. As she went through the heavy glass doors she found herself in a high brown-walled foyer with worn tile flooring and a massive oak staircase twisting up out of sight. The building smelled of dust and old dreams.

She was studying a small, glassed-in directory on the wall when someone came out of an office door to the left. "Miss Baxter?"

Ruth turned. The man was tall, beefy, with short curly red hair that receded. He wore tight white Levis and a red checkered cotton shirt with the sleeves rolled part way up brawny fore-arms. His pointed, heeled boots matched the great silver longhorn buckle on his belt. She guessed his age at forty.

"Mrs. Baxter," she corrected him automatically.

The man grinned and held out a thick hand. "My name is Vachon. Chuck Vachon. I'm the undersheriff for this part of the county. Al Crewser called me from the drugstore and said to watch for you, give you all the help you needed. He says you're from back East and you're checking on your family tree."

Ruth let him briefly mangle her hand in his great paw. "That's very kind of you." She didn't like Vachon.

"Checking on a man name of John Bartelson, I hear."

7

"That's right."

"Well, I swan. I never ran into a family-tree hunter before. Are they all as pretty as you?" He leered at her in his nice-boy way.

Ruth coolly ignored it. "Old city tax certificates and records of census, if any, would be helpful, Mr. Vachon. And if there's a city court—"

"Except for traffic," Vachon cut in, "everything likely to help you will be in the basement. That's where we've got all our old records. They're all part of the library, you see."

"Will you direct me, please?"

"Mighty fine!" He took her arm. "You just come with me, little lady, and we'll have you all fixed up in no time."

Gritting her teeth, Ruth let him escort her down the back stairs. The basement corridor was narrow, lighted by bare bulbs in porcelain sockets set into jungles of pipes and conduits. At least it was cooler. Vachon led her through double glazed doors and they were in air conditioning again.

It was the library. She was agreeably surprised. A single long room, about thirty feet wide and twice that in length, it was starkly utilitarian and very neat. Shelves of books extended straight back from a front reception-checkout desk. She saw a card file and metal shelving along the inside wall containing old manuscripts and newspaper files. There were also tall boxes farther back that hinted of minimal archival holdings. Fluorescent fixtures, obviously new, hung over two long blond reading tables in front of the counter. There were library association posters on the bare plaster walls.

"Anybody home?" Vachon called, startlingly loud in the quiet.

"Just a minute," a male voice called from the back.

Vachon went to the counter, crossed booted feet and leaned heavy hands on the immaculate Formica. He winked at Ruth.

Ruth remained by the door. She was very irritated. Vachon's approach was so crude she was not equipped to put it down.

In a moment the man who had answered Vachon's call came from the back, carrying a stack of books. He was a pleasant surprise: young—her age or younger—dark-haired, slender, and not at all bad-looking. He had quick dark eyes and a full beard that she rather liked.

Putting the books down on the counter, he brushed his hands on his open-necked white shirt and gave Vachon a look that was curiously neither friendly nor hostile but perfectly, guardedly neutral.

"Doug," Vachon said, grinning, clasping his shoulder with a big hand, "I've got a visitor. She's from back East and she wants a look-see at some of the old stuff for work on a family tree."

The man behind the counter gave Ruth a quick, keen glance. "All right." His tone, she noticed, gave absolutely no hint of his reaction.

She walked to the counter and extended her hand. "I'm Ruth Baxter."

"Doug Bennett." His handshake was firm, yet curiously neutral.

She explained what little she knew about John Bartelson.

"I may be able to help you," he said.

"Are you interested in genealogy yourself?" she asked.

His eyes were flat. "Not really."

Vachon said, "I think she wants some old city records, Doug. How about trotting those out for her?"

Doug Bennett nodded. "Fine. I think the old county history may be helpful, too. And the early county-court material."

"County court?" Ruth said. "I thought—"

"Noble was the county seat until 1937," Doug Bennett told her. "Most of the old records are still here. The library acts as custodian."

"That's marvelous. I ought to be able to find everything available."

"You don't want to rummage around in them old boxes!" Vachon argued. "Boy, they're filthy dirty and all messed up."

"I've been cataloguing," Doug Bennett said quietly. "I can put my hands on most of the things she'll need. No problem."

"She doesn't want any of that," Vachon argued. "She wants—"

"On the contrary," Ruth said coolly. "I think Mr. Bennett understands precisely the materials I need, even though genealogy may bore him personally."

"It doesn't bore me," Doug Bennett said. "It simply isn't a factor."

"All right. I still trust you. Will you check your holdings?"

He turned, expressionless, to begin checking index cards. Ruth watched him. He was quick and sure. He had good hands, blunt-fingered yet gentle. She wanted to ask what he was doing in a basement library in a dying town in southeastern Oklahoma.

"I'll get some of these and be right back," he told her.

Vachon sighed, walked over to a table and sat down.

Waiting, Ruth wondered why no one had mentioned that Noble had been the county seat. Hadn't she mentioned county records to the druggist? And had she imagined it, or was Vachon too eager to give her only city files? Was she making it up, or was there resistance here?

There was, at least, no resistance from Doug Bennett despite his frown. First he brought out three volumes, which turned out to be an old high-school annual dated 1935, a hand-bound edition of a typewritten *History of Archer County,* dated 1924, and a mimeographed list of biographies and genealogies in Oklahoma libraries, compiled by the DAR.

"I'll get the court materials," he told her. "You can start on these."

Vachon reached for the old high-school yearbook. "I'll check this 'un."

"There's no need for that," Ruth told him. "I can do it for myself."

Vachon grinned and winked at her. "Don't have a thing in the world to do until quitting time. Might jus' as well educate myself a little." He hunched over the annual and began turning pages.

Puzzled by his seeming interest, Ruth nevertheless took out her note-taking materials and ballpoint and began skimming the DAR list. It was quick work and fruitless. There had never been a Bartelson genealogy. That didn't surprise her. She put the listing aside and turned to the county history.

The first part was general history, and she flipped pages. She saw, however, that the manuscript began individual biographies on manuscript page 106. They were alphabetized. She flipped through the B's, expecting nothing, and then got one of those little thrills that only a genealogist could appreciate.

On page 117 she found:

BARTELSON, *John. Businessman, Noble. John Bartelson came to Archer Cty. soon after statehood and opened Bartelson's Drygoods Co. Originally from the east, he served with the U.S. Army in Europe during the great war and returned this cty afterward, continuing his business. On May 17, 1914, he married* Gladys Streder, *whose parents, Adam and Sarah Streder, came to the territory from Alabama at a very early day. John Bartelson's father, Jepton Bartelson, came from Massachusetts to New York City and was a clothier. John Bartelson was elected to Noble Town Board, 1920, and now serves on the town school board. He enlarged his business in 1921 and is considered Noble's leading drygoods merchant.*

Ruth read the entire entry, brief as it was, twice. It gave her considerable information that she hadn't had before, the most surprising being John Bartelson's marriage. Hadn't Alvin Crewser, at the drugstore, told her there had never been a family?

It was a problem she would worry about later. Uncapping her pen, she began copying the entry in its entirety.

Vachon shoved the yearbook aside. "Nothing in this. You find something there?" He leaned toward her.

Ruth shook her head and covered the page partially with her hand. "Just general information about the county."

"How come you to copy it, then?"

"General information," she told him crisply.

Vachon frowned at her. "Nothing about him, though?"

"No, I'm afraid not. But this will help my uncle add a little general detail and make the entry more interesting, even if we have little biography."

Vachon sniffed and leaned back in his chair as Doug Bennett came from the back carrying a stack of dusty old red courthouse ledgers. Ruth copied quickly and efficiently.

Why had she lied to Vachon? She did not know. She only understood a generalized impulse to caution. Her impulses were seldom wrong, even when—as now—she did not fully understand them. She wondered what it was about this town and its people that aroused her defense mechanisms.

She told herself—again—that she was being silly.

CHAPTER 2

The clock showed almost 5:30. Except for an occasional comment, the three of them had been silent in the library for a long time. Most of the old books were piled on the edge of the table. Ruth had finished with her last ledger and was frowning at her notes. Doug Bennett smoked a cigarette. In a moment Vachon whacked the cover on his ledger book, sending a faint cloud of dust across the table.

"Done!"

"Nothing in that one?" Ruth asked.

Vachon shrugged. "Afraid not."

She looked at Doug. "Is there anything more?"

"I think not," he told her.

"What time do you close?"

"Thirty minutes ago."

"I am sorry."

Doug gave her a faint smile. She was easy to smile at. There were no women like this in Noble. Despite her evident interest in a kind of research he personally considered fusty, he liked her quite a lot after their two hours together. She was not only very lovely, with that long dark hair and her wide-set green eyes; she was sharp. The way she held herself, the manner in which she absently touched her hair, the intent, serious, open quality of her gaze said there was a good mind there, one with a sophistication he seldom met. A gag line from an old Limeliters song crossed his memory: *Clean mind, clean body.* In her case it was different: quick mind, stunning body. Watch it, Bennett. She's a married woman and you're a broken-down Vietnam vet with nothing on your mind but being left alone.

He said, "No problem staying open a little late. We open again from seven till nine most nights."

"And I've kept you here during the time you have to eat," Ruth said. "I do apologize."

Vachon said, "Public service. No sweat. And you got some mighty fine information, too, didn't you?"

Ruth consulted her notes. "I certainly know a lot more than I did before. He must have come here early in 1912, because we have the record of his buying the property at 226 West Main Street in July of that year. Then in 1918 he went into the Army, but he was back in 1920 when he was named to the town board. In 1921 he sold the property at 226 West Main and bought the larger store next door, at 228–230. In 1923 he was executor of Clyde Finnigan's will, in 1924 he was elected to the school board, in 1925 he was sued for assault by a customer named J. R. Willis but was acquitted in a jury trial, in 1926 he was named under-sheriff." She paused and looked at Doug. "Then we have that bad thing you found, about his filing for bankruptcy in 1931, and then we have his death on December 8, 1935, and the coroner's jury verdict that it was suicide, a self-inflicted gunshot wound."

Doug nodded. Uncovering the old tragedy had surprised him. "At least now your uncle will know."

"I'd say so!" Vachon grinned. "We got *lots* of good stuff!"

Doug felt a stab of irritation, but said nothing.

Ruth collected her papers into the small attaché case. "I do want to thank you again," she told him as if Vachon weren't even there.

"Don't mention it."

"I may stop by in the morning, if I have time, to look over old newspapers. I want to get pictures of where his store used to be, and then I'll probably go to the cemetery. But I may have an hour or two before I have to start for Dallas."

"We'll be closed in the morning," he told her.

"Oh," she said, disappointed.

He wondered if she always got her own way. He realized he wanted to see her again, and that irritated him. He curbed the impulse to explain why he would be closed.

Vachon asked, "Can you find your way out, little lady?"

Ruth's expression was a cross between irritation and amusement. "I think so, Mr. Vachon." She turned to Doug. "Again—thank you."

Doug nodded but said nothing.

She hesitated, then walked to the door and went out. She was damned good-looking. Doug listened to her footsteps recede. He was angry with himself and did not know exactly why.

"Mighty pretty woman," Vachon said in the silence.

Doug began gathering up the things on the table. He had never liked Vachon, and the lawman's crude flirtation had embarrassed him.

"Like to know if you hear anything more from her," Vachon said now.

"Why?"

Vachon's beefy face was slack, and his eyes had the quality of old glass. "No reason. Just want to be helpful."

"Interested in genealogy?"

Vachon leered. "Izzat what you call it? I was just trying to get a peek down the front of her blouse at those tits."

"That's one of your better qualities, Vachon. You always manage to put things in the perspective of the lowest common denominator."

"Is that supposed to be funny?"

"No. I know when I'm out of my class."

"Well, just let me know if she comes back, or anything like that. Right?"

"Why are you so interested in her?"

"Look," Vachon snapped in a different tone. "Cooperate. Right?"

Doug looked up at him and saw the flecks of anger in his eyes.

"Because," Vachon said, "you're a town boy, right? You're a

good old boy. We all know that. You've got your little job and you send off for these hippie-peacenik magazines and let your hair grow all over your face, but we don't say a word. Right? Live and let live. Right? The town owes you. You went over there and fought those Communists in Vietnam and even got a medal. So we let you do your thing. But you owe the town a little, too, buddy. Like when the law tells you to cooperate, you cooperate. You don't pull any wise-ass beatnik shit. Right?"

Doug continued to look at Vachon for a long moment. For a lot of reasons, many of them irrational, he felt a very strong impulse to take him, right then, right there. The Ranger-Beret training was not that far behind him; he could do it. Vachon was a formidable man, a hard one. But Doug thought he could take him, and he wanted to do just that.

But he hadn't come back for that. He had declared his own peace. He wasn't going to fight anybody's battles. He wasn't going to fight even his own. He was going to stay here, awhile at least, and hope the things inside him would heal.

He said with a little smile, "I always aim to please, Chuck."

Vachon grinned and clapped him heavily on the back. "That's my boy! See you tomorrow."

The door slammed behind him.

Still angry, Doug locked the door and carried a stack of the ledgers to the back tables where they customarily stayed. Then he went into the storage room and opened the little refrigerator. He got out the cold meat and mustard and milk, pulled the loaf of bread out of the file cabinet and sat at the rolltop desk to make his supper.

Ruth Baxter's visit had been a pleasant, if unsettling, diversion. He wondered what sort of trip was taking her to Dallas. She was in business of some kind, probably, not a stay-at-home, and stopping off here to help an uncle on the genealogy. That was a kindness. He wished she didn't have the kindness. Without it he could have imagined she was cold, and there would have been no vague regret.

Eating his sandwich, he thought about other sources of information he might have in the small library. He might be back in Noble as a sort of one-man gesture of dismay and desperation, a no-symbol dropout who only wanted some time to forget the smoke, the blood, the babies crying beside gut-ripped mothers, the crisply efficient senior officers lecturing about body counts and reducing the native will to aid "the enemy"—he might want *nothing* right now but to be left alone while he tried to work it out. But Ruth Baxter's little project strangely fascinated him, and he found himself wishing he could help. At least it was an innocent hobby. At least there was no killing in it and no motivation to clamber over someone else's body to a cash register in the sky.

The newspaper files, Doug thought, were a good possibility. He wondered if they contained anything.

Leaving his sandwich on the table, he got down the weekly files for 1931 through 1935, figuring an obituary was the best bet.

He first opened the 1935 volume, far to the back, to December. Knowing John Bartelson's death date from the court record, it was easy to bracket the two issues an obit might have been in.

He turned a page and there it was.

It was more prominent than he would have expected, and the headline shocked him.

NOBLE BUSINESSMAN
ALL-STATE STAR'S FATHER,
FOUND DEAD AT HOME

John A. Bartelson, retired Noble businessman and father of Noble High School's All-State fullback of two years ago, Press Bartelson, was found dead in his home, 711 Fawnee Ave., last Tuesday.

John Bartelson was 45.

Owner of a clothing store on Main Street until about three years ago, he was a member of the Noble Town Board in the 1920's and later served on the school board. He was undersheriff from 1926 to 1928, when business problems caused him to resign. In 1924 he was Oklahoma state trap-shooting champion.

His son, Press, led the 1932 and 1933 Noble Broncos to

consecutive state championships. Press was captain of the team and selected small-school All-State fullback in 1933. After attending Oklahoma A&M College for one year, Press returned to Noble and is the owner of a sporting goods store here.

John Bartelson came to Noble soon after statehood. He was a member of the Methodist Church and Noble Boosters Club. In addition to his son, he is survived by his wife Gladys, of the home.

Services pend with Lucky Funeral Home.

Doug didn't know quite what to make of it. From what he recalled of information from the court records, one or two minor items were wrong. That was to be expected in the tiny Noble weekly. The line about "retirement" at such an early age was a familiar Depression euphemism, and the little paper could hardly have been expected to say the deceased had evidently blown his own brains out.

The angle he couldn't understand, however, was the existence of a son named Press—a local hero, apparently, in the mid-thirties.

Fascinated now, Doug ignored his sandwich on the desk and went to the back tables outside where the ledgers and other documents were stacked. He pulled up a chair and started back through them. Things weren't making sense, and he intended to discover why.

From the window of the Cherokee Motel, the view was of a U-shaped asphalt parking lot that contained only two cars: an old Chevrolet sedan parked beside the pine-paneled front office, and Ruth's new Vega in front of her unit, which was along the back row of units facing toward the street. The VACANCY sign glowed red in the draped window of the motel office, and at the corner, in blackness, a traffic signal blinked green, then red, and then green again, signaling only ghost traffic. The air conditioner in the back wall chuffed weakly against the wet, omnipresent heat. With a small shiver, Ruth Baxter turned away from the window, letting the thin green drape fall back in place.

She had eaten a soggy sandwich, accompanied by a weak cup of coffee, at the truck stop two blocks away. Now the ancient Motorola in the corner, the sound turned down, flicked black and white pictures of a network comedy. It was just past nine.

Wearing a light robe, she walked to the bed and looked down at the materials strewn on the faded pink chenille bedspread: her notebook, the Xeroxed charts from her uncle's materials about the family, her opened attaché case, the Canon camera, the road map, the copy of the latest weekly newspaper she had picked up downtown.

She had gotten, she thought, precious little information. But she knew Uncle Carl would be pleased. It was probably enough: proof that John Bartelson had come here, lived his life and died. The dates were definite.

She wished distantly that she hadn't found that Bartelson had died by his own hand. There was something still depressing about the picture that the scant facts portrayed: a man coming west, as they said, to make good, and doing all the "right" things—serving in the Army, opening his own business, serving the community. But for Bartelson it had all gone sour. Ruth tried to imagine how it must have been, staking one's life in this remote place, walking every day under these brooding old trees, feeling the heat of late summers suck the energy out of every pore, watching forces that no one could understand take away everything that had been worked for, saved, built against the future.

She shivered again, for no reason, and hugged her arms about herself. She did not like this place. She would be glad to leave it.

The motel unit depressed her. It was an old motel now, juke-box-modern, the room about twelve feet square with a garish little green tile cubicle walled off in one corner for an open closet and bath that had only a bare lavatory, rust-stained bowl and cement-floored cubicle for a shower that was covered by a slightly mildewed yellow plastic shower curtain. The ceiling was acoustical tile long ago gone yellow and stained in the corners by random rain leakage. The walls, covered with shiny yellow paneling that was supposed to look like knotty pine, were wavy where the panels had warped and pulled loose. The brown tile floor needed washing and waxing. The furniture consisted of the cracked blond bed with its pink coverlet, two straight-backed mahogany chairs with dark green plastic seat cushions, a mahogany dresser that seemed to lean slightly to one side, a blond end table beside the bed with an urn-type lamp and square black telephone without a dial.

She was looking directly at the telephone when it rang, making her jump.

She picked up the receiver.

"Mrs. Baxter?" the voice said, and she recognized him. "This is Doug Bennett. At the library."

"Yes," Ruth said. Surely he was cooler than to—

"I've uncovered some additional information that I think will interest you."

"Oh?" She heard the tinge of skepticism in her own voice. If Vachon had called and tried this old trick, she might not have been so surprised. She hadn't expected it from Doug Bennett. "What kind of information?"

"I'd rather not talk about it on the telephone. Would you like to come down to the library?"

"Isn't the library closed by now?"

"Yes, but I can stay here and wait for you."

"It's late," she said. Although she knew she had allowed the coolness to be clear in her voice this time, she told herself she might be misjudging him. "I've driven a long way today," she added.

"Well, I could come by there if you'd prefer."

She felt sharp disappointment. Maybe it was inevitable that they would react like this. A woman alone, traveling far from home. As a target she was simply too obvious to overlook. Even for a man like him. And yet she had thought he was better than that.

"I don't think you need to come by here," she said.

"How will you get this information?"

"Do I really need it, Mr. Bennett?" she asked nastily.

There was a pause and then he said, "I see. You think—"

"Thank you for calling."

"Your man had a son."

"*What?*"

"Bartelson," Doug Bennett said, and now there was the sound of cold ashes in his tone, "had a son. His name was Press. I have the documentation if you're interested. I'm supposed to go to McAlester in the morning for a bookmobile meeting, but I can leave my notes with the city clerk and someone can let you into the library if you want to do any further checking on it yourself before you leave."

Ruth sank to the edge of the bed. Her hands went to the Xeroxed charts and she turned over the one that showed her uncle's family line. "John Bartelson had a *brother* named Press," she said with a tremor of discovery. "He was born in 1885, died in 1924. If John Bartelson came out here and had a son and named him after his brother—"

"This Press was born on November first, 1915," Doug Bennett said. The same flat, bitter tone was in his voice. "I'll leave the information with the clerk."

"Wait! Why didn't we find this earlier? Why didn't anyone *tell* me?"

"I have no idea. The clerk will have the information I've gathered. I hope it's helpful."

"You won't be back before I leave? I wanted to ask—"

"It may be early afternoon, Mrs. Baxter. Possibly I'll see you then, possibly you'll be gone by then. You have no more need to see me, and I certainly have no need to see you again, so it makes no difference."

Ruth winced. She had been wrong and he had read her with crystal clarity. She deserved that.

She said, "I've changed my mind. Can I still come down there?"

"I think you were right. It is late. This is all written down anyway."

He's proud, she thought, and now he's a little puffed up and bitter. She had been a bitch again.

"Look, I am sorry. Couldn't I come down now and see what you've found and talk about it?"

His tone didn't change. He was angry. "Whatever you think."

"I'll be there," she told him, "in just a few minutes."

The distance was too short for the Vega's air conditioning to start working well, so she drove with the window down. Night had done little to dispel the intense heat, and the air that flowed inside the car felt like the draft of a cooling furnace. The streets were empty, and when she turned onto Main, the only signs of life were three cars parked beside the little café-tavern on the corner. The broken street lay empty, like the set of an abandoned movie, and in the crystal sky overhead there were a billion unbelievable stars.

Lights shone behind the frosted basement windows of the library, and when she went up the stairs to the front entrance of the old building, the door opened and Doug Bennett was standing there.

"It's locked at this time of night," he explained. "I watched for your lights."

"There isn't much night life," she observed, stepping into the black foyer as he relocked the front doors.

"They still claim four thousand population for Noble," he told her, leading her lightly by the arm toward the faintly lighted stairs. "But I'd guess the figure is about half that now, really."

They were tight with each other, almost angry, and talking about anything to avoid silence.

"What happened to the town?"

"The Depression. A lot of towns in Oklahoma never came back. The economic thing ruined businesses downtown, and then the Dust Bowl days got the farmers."

They were going down the stairs.

"But this area is so hilly and wooded, it's hard to imagine it as part of the Dust Bowl."

"The rainfall here is six times what it is in counties to the west. But there were a few years when it didn't rain much at all, they say. Even the people who could raise a few things, marginally, had no markets. Texas and New Mexico blew into Oklahoma, and Oklahoma dirt blew all the way to Pennsylvania. It hit everywhere. You know that."

"And there was nothing else," Ruth mused, stepping into the library, "to fall back on."

"No. The coal mines had played out long before."

"Coal? In Oklahoma?"

"Southeastern Oklahoma had tremendous coal deposits. Some areas still do. There are four abandoned coal mines—big ones —not ten miles from where we're standing. Farther south and east, coal was a big industry long before statehood. Those areas have big Polish and Czech populations even today from the years when immigrants flocked out here to work in the mines."

"I had no idea."

Doug motioned to her. "The books are in the back." As he led the way between stacks he told her, "Noble wasn't always like this. When your relative came here, the population was probably more than fifteen thousand. It was booming. The future probably appeared unlimited." He paused at a table where ledgers and newspaper files lay open. "But then the things began to happen. It dwindled and kept going downhill. The young people were smart; they left. Some people stayed. Now there aren't many young people here, and they leave as soon as they can. The ones who stay have nothing—no real hopes. They hang on. They're like a terminal patient, waiting. And the waiting makes them shrivel and turn in and get mean and hate, but they hide the hate, but it comes out." He took a deep breath. "It comes out."

"I was hateful a while ago," she told him.

He looked surprised. "Forget it."

"All right. But I'm sorry."

He smiled briefly. It was the first time, and it made him younger. "Let me show you what I've found."

In quick order he let her read, and take notes from, the newspaper obituary. There was also a story from 1924, telling how her kinsman had won the state trapshooting competition in Guthrie, an aspect of his life she had not suspected. Finally he showed her the record of Press Bartelson's birth, properly recorded in the old county records on November 3, 1915, showing a son born November 1, the name given as Press Jepton Bartelson, the parents John August Bartelson and Gladys Eva Bartelson.

When her note-taking was finished, Ruth looked at the new information. It was considerably different from what she had expected—or been told—only a few hours ago.

"But why didn't we find this birth registration earlier?" she asked. "Didn't we go through this book?"

"It was on the table. One of us went through it."

"I didn't. Did you?"

"No."

She met his eyes. "Then Chuck Vachon did."

"He missed it."

"Do you really think so?"

"What other explanation is there?"

"He could have seen it and passed over it intentionally," Ruth said.

"Why would he do that?"

"I don't know."

They looked at each other. She saw that something was on his mind.

"Well," he said finally, "you've found it now."

So the idea was dismissed. "If he's recorded in the newspaper as an All-State football player," she said, "why didn't we see any mention of it in those high-school annuals? Didn't we look at the right years?"

Doug lit a cigarette and inhaled deeply. "I got those out, of course, because local merchants always advertise, and I thought we might find an old ad for Bartelson's store. But it occurred to me that we should have spotted something about the boy, even going through casually. So I looked back at the '34 and '35 volumes."

"And?" Ruth was aware of the tension in her voice.

"Some of the pages had been torn out."

"The pages about Press Bartelson?"

Doug's forehead wrinkled. "Until I came back, the library was a disaster area. Practically anyone could get a key and come in and shuffle through things on his own. A lot of the old records have been vandalized."

"So you think it's an accident?"

"I don't know."

"I came into town," Ruth told him, angry for no reason she could adequately define, "and I was told John Bartelson never married. But that was a lie. I was told there were no children. But that was a lie. I was given to believe there would be no records. But that was a lie. Now we know he did marry and had a son named Press. But there's no sign in any of these records that he ever existed! What happened to him? What happened to John Bartelson's wife? What's going *on* around here?"

"You know how old records can get fouled up," Doug began. "Even in a well-run courthouse—"

Up front, beyond the stacks, the doors to the corridor rattled and then opened.

Frowning, Doug left Ruth standing there and hurried up between the stacks.

A voice boomed, "Anybody in this place?" Vachon.

Remaining where she was, Ruth heard Doug reply, "I'm here."

"Seen the lights. Thought I'd check."

"I'm working a little late, that's all."

"Seen the little New York lady's car parked out there. She come back by any chance? She in here someplace, too?"

"I'm here," Ruth said coolly, walking down the line of stacks to a point where he could see her.

Vachon, his face glistening with sweat and his shirt plastered to his powerful torso by moisture, stood just inside the corridor doors. His eyes had a sheen to them. She saw he was slightly drunk.

He grimaced. "Well, I swan. I thought you was all through pokin' around in here."

"I forgot my cigarette lighter. I was lucky enough to catch Mr. Bennett before he closed up."

Vachon glanced at the big military-style watch on his thick wrist. "Mighty far past closin' time now."

"We've been talking."

"Lookin' up more stuff, too, maybe?"

"There's nothing more to look up," Ruth told him levelly. "We did all the records earlier, don't you remember?"

"Sure," Vachon said, and his grin had a slanted, Mephistophelian quality. "Well, I sure hate to break up your gabfest, but it's mighty late and the building ought to be shut down proper. You all about finished here?"

Doug replied, "We'll be through shortly. I'll lock up."

"I'll just wait outside in my car," Vachon told him.

"No need," Doug said, his eyes bleak.

"Jus' part of the job. No problem. Got to keep an eye out, you know. I'll jus' wait outside. Don't you all be too long now." He gave Ruth a look, turned to the door, staggered slightly and went out, leaving it open behind him.

Doug shot Ruth a warning look and then said, "Well, we'd better close up. I'm glad I was still here so you could get your lighter."

Ruth nodded and said nothing. She waited while he went to the back. She heard him closing books and moving things around. In a moment he was back.

"Ready?" he asked softly.

She clutched the notebooks to her side. "I don't understand any of this. I want to talk about it. Something is—"

"We can go to the café and have a cup of coffee."

"I don't want to go to that café and have people watching me."

"What do you suggest?"

"You can come to my room."

"If I had suggested that an hour ago, you would have called Vachon."

"It isn't an hour ago," she shot back, "and I'm beginning to see who I can trust and who I can't. *Something* strange is going on around here, and you know it as well as I do. Will you come so we can talk about it?"

"It won't look very good," he said dubiously.

"Oh my God," she said wearily.

Suddenly he smiled with a touch of irony. "My car is parked at the side. I'll follow you out there."

"You *do* know something strange is going on," she said.

"I'm not sure any of it means a thing. But I'm interested enough to talk about it. Maybe together we can figure out what the big secret is supposed to be—if there is one."

Satisfied, Ruth nodded and followed him out of the black

building. She walked down to her car and saw a black Ford sedan parked two slots away. There was a figure in the car. Vachon. She saw the shadow of his torso turn to watch her as she walked to the Vega, got in, pressed the door locks down with a firm stab, started the engine and backed into the street. She saw Doug Bennett's headlights come out of the side street and turn in behind her as she drove slowly up past the darkened drugstore. The headlights of Doug's car were oddly reassuring.

CHAPTER 3

Sometimes Doug Bennett surprised himself.

Following the taillights of the Vega toward the motel, he wondered seriously what in the hell he was trying to prove. The lady was not for playing; he was sure of that, and satisfied that he would have had it no other way, even though the suggestion kept flitting around the edges of his consciousness. This, he thought, was because she was so startlingly attractive and he instinctively liked her so much. He had known some of her type: the career girl who was no longer a girl but a full-blown woman, who said she wanted only to be treated as a man's equal and yet would never be an equal because no man with anything between his legs could ever quite forget the attraction. Yet Doug sensed that Ruth Baxter did not consciously trade on her sex, even though she was intelligent and candid enough to know it was an advantage. This was part of what he liked about her. She was not phony. Once or twice at the library she had smiled at him in a way that was not a come-hither, yet recognized tacitly that they were not neuter equals. She carried her sex nicely, living with it and comfortable with it and not trying to pretend that it was either some kind of handicap or handy club. Her crispness, he sensed, was based on a hard shrewdness and real interior toughness. But there was that feeling underneath that she was a fully functioning woman and anything but ashamed of it. She would always be a lady, he thought, and formidable. In the bedroom she might not be a lady at all.

He had never met quite such a sharp yet relaxed combination of keen self-sufficiency and modifying natural femininity. Fire and ice. Robert Frost hadn't written those words in this context, but they fit. Doug was fascinated and wished he could know her truly. She would not run out of surprises.

But among the other things he had promised himself a year ago, he thought now, was that he would never—*ever*—get himself into that kind of situation with a woman again. Linda had had a trace of Ruth Baxter's wit, a touch of her self-reliance, perhaps a fraction of her aura of complexity and fascination. Less a woman, Doug thought, and yet she had almost managed to destroy him with no such intent whatsoever.

One day, maybe, he would get over it. He was not over it yet and he knew it. There were a lot of things he hadn't gotten over. He was still just a little of a cripple. Any kind of a relationship with Ruth Baxter was not only wildly unlikely but potentially disastrous.

So that part was out.

Why was he going along, then? Boredom? Curiousity? The old perverse streak?

All of them, he decided.

He *had* been bored. Despite his insistence to himself that he didn't want a damned thing out of life, at least not now, Ruth Baxter's visit today had proven to him, by his reaction, that the rut had been getting too deep. And there was no doubt, too, that his curiosity was piqued. She had some points. It looked increasingly as if somebody had almost conspired to hide the fact that Press Bartelson had ever existed.

Which made no sense at all, and only a fool would pursue the matter.

Enter his perversity. All he needed was to arouse the enmity of *anyone* around Noble right now. They distrusted him enough, with his beard and shaggy hair. He had no real friends in Noble and knew it. But they hadn't put any pressure on him to leave. Not yet. As long as he was a good little boy and straightened up their library and minded his own business, they might pay him his $90 a week indefinitely. That was just the way he wanted it: no friends, no obligations, no complications, nothing.

So only perversity could be getting him involved. He had to agree with her that it appeared someone was trying to conceal something about John Bartelson or his family. But it wasn't likely to mean much even if they found out what it was, and he suspected she was interested mainly because she liked to have her own way. All beautiful women had a selfish streak.

So the hell with it, he thought again. So he was crazy.

He followed the Vega to the motel and pulled in right beside it in the back of the U-shaped lot, aware as he got out that there had been a movement at the drapes of the front office. He wondered sarcastically if they took infra-red movies.

"Here we are," Ruth Baxter said, unlocking the door of her unit.

Doug went in. "It's not exactly the Ritz," he observed.

"At least it's cool."

Doug sat in one of the straight chairs in the corner and watched her move her notebooks and other gear off the bed. She looked trim and nice and thoroughly like a professional woman, although her dress was summery and she was bare-legged. He found he had as much curiosity about her as about the circumstances they had uncovered.

"I don't have any liquor," she told him, "but there's some old coffee in this Thermos."

"Fine."

She poured and handed him a plastic cup, then took the chair facing him. "What do you think I should do?" she asked directly.

"I think you ought to take the information you have and get the hell out," he said bluntly.

"But there was a son, and he was prominent. Now there's no real record. I've been lied to, and that bothers me a lot. I should simply leave it?"

"I would."

"Why?"

"Because it might all be just a mixup. The records might have been legitimately lost or overlooked. He probably moved away. People forget. The entire thing can be explained. You have the information you came for. You have dates and information. Your uncle—is that the relationship?—your uncle can write down in his manuscript that there was a son, record unknown. You can't chase the family tree back to Adam. Let it go."

"I'm not built like that," she said, and a stubborn little furrow showed across her forehead. "I hate to leave it now."

"Well, Press Bartelson isn't around now. I checked the telephone books for the last ten years. He either died or moved away. You could spend months here and possibly find no more than you already have. People are tight-lipped around here. They don't trust strangers. They don't even trust me, and I'm a town boy."

"What are you doing here in this town?" she asked suddenly, her head tilted as she stared at him with genuine interest.

Feeling guarded, he shrugged. "Making a living."

"Are you a professional librarian?"

"I have a degree, if that's what you mean. University of Oklahoma. Library science."

"You came back here after college?"

He drained the coffee cup, which was cool and bitter. "After Vietnam."

"You were in the Army."

"Four years."

"When were you in Vietnam?"

"A long time." Doug stretched his legs, not liking the conversation. "A *long* time. Sixty-six to seventy."

"My husband was there in sixty-eight," she said.

"Is he still in the Army?"

"He was killed."

"There?"

"Yes."

"I'm sorry."

She smiled. "So am I."

It was unsatisfactory. Her dress was pale yellow, sleeveless, cut short on her legs. They were good legs, not model-slender but more substantial, and her sandals emphasized their allure.

Doug felt himself pulled toward her, wanting her, thinking how those fine legs would be strong around a man. He didn't want to think about that. He hated that part of himself.

He said, "This isn't getting to the business of the missing files, though."

But she wouldn't let it alone. "Why were you in Vietnam so long?"

"What difference does it make?" he asked harshly. Then he knew how it sounded. She was just trying to be nice. He added wearily, "I re-enlisted and volunteered to stay. I was still thinking maybe there was something we could do—win it."

"I see." But her eyes showed quiet surprise.

"I must have been one of the last people in the world to see what was really going on," Doug added, not wanting to talk about it, yet goaded somehow by her quiet, by the lure of those legs. He slapped his thigh. "Let's just say I got in a couple of genuine battles, worked up a nice hate, got a medal and thought medals meant something."

"But now you're back here. You changed your mind."

"I had a hassle with my captain. If I hadn't, I might never have gotten out. I'm no heroic liberal martyr."

"Do you always sell yourself so short?"

"I try to avoid deluding myself."

"How did you get out of the Army if you re-enlisted? I thought —"

His anger burst through—at himself, at her. "I was a fool, that's how. There was a demonstration. The Army likes only one kind of a fool, the kind who's insane in the *Army* way. So I was discharged. Now are we going to talk about your John Bartelson or not?"

She stood, a little pale before his outburst. "I was prying. I'm sorry."

"It doesn't matter," he muttered. "Forget it. I'm sorry too. Now look: what about these records?"

She took a deep breath. "I don't know what to do."

"Let it go."

"Maybe I will." After his outburst she was quieter, somehow

withdrawn and different with him now, as if aware of him in a new way. Her slight movements showed she was aware of the room, the motel room and their aloneness. She added, "It's probably just my stubbornness anyway. People in small towns like to make secrets of nothing. I'm a stranger. Probably it all amounts to nothing, and I have enough for Uncle Carl."

Doug nodded, agreeing outwardly, although it cost him something. "Vachon will be pleased."

"Is he *always* like that?" she asked, leaning forward.

"No. Sometimes he acts a little crude."

She surprised him. A little barking laugh broke her composure. "I can't imagine that! He's so suave!"

Doug had to grin. "He was on his best behavior for you."

"I don't know how you stand it here," she said more seriously. "You're smarter than that. Why haven't you gone to a city?"

"I may one day."

"But a little place like this." She made a face. "It's so shabby—closed in. I don't—"

"I know," he agreed, but his face heated. "On the other hand, tourists from the East wouldn't have anything to laugh at if we didn't operate all these little gas stops out here in the wasteland beween the Hudson and Los Angeles."

She saw her mistake and her face changed. "I didn't mean it to sound that way."

"I have a tendency to overreact," he admitted. "I get a little sick of people telling me what a pit Noble is. Local people tell me that to impress me with how cosmopolitan they are. Visitors tell me the same thing to prove how superior they are. A lot of people like to play the game. You can get real clubby, making fun of the town and building up your own sense of superiority in the process."

"I wasn't playing that game," she protested.

"Oh, hell," he muttered wearily, "I know that. It is a lousy little town. It's a poor town in a poor county in a poor section of a poor state in a poor region. But as long as I live here, let's face it, I'm living here *by choice*. I'm not trapped. Either I live with it and accept it or I get out. I don't stay but pretend I'm too good for the place just to impress somebody."

Her serious eyes studied him. "You're very proud."

"No," he grunted disgustedly. "I've just got a very big mouth."

"You're selling yourself short again."

"You don't know me."

There was something behind her eyes. "I suppose I don't."

Meeting her gaze, Doug felt a pang of internal electricity.

He knew she felt it too. He could get up now and walk to her, without saying anything at all, and take her in his arms. They were alone and didn't know each other well, but he could do that, and she would allow it. And then he could undress her and feel those arms and legs around him and see her eyes change as it happened.

The thought was so vivid that it shook him badly.

They were silent. She did not move, standing there by the bed.

Outside, a truck rumbled past. The sound broke the moment.

Doug got to his feet and started for the door. "I'll be going to that meeting. If I don't get back before you leave, good luck to you."

"Thanks." She smiled, but the tension was still there in the way she moved guardedly toward the door, not getting too close. "I may be here long enough to say goodbye."

"Maybe so." It was a lie, he thought. He would not be back before she left, and they both knew it. "I'll probably see you then," he said.

"I still wish I could understand why that man at the drugstore said what he did," she said. "And the other things."

And he understood this, too, and marveled at it. She was re-establishing distance.

"Maybe you'll clear it all up in the morning," he suggested, opening the door to the heat.

"Maybe so," she said and smiled.

He looked back at her. "Good night."

She closed the door quickly behind him.

He walked to his car, started it and drove away. That, he told himself, was that. She would try to find more information in the morning, but it wasn't likely she would find any. He would get back from McAlester in the afternoon and she would be gone. Possibly he had imagined the feeling between them anyway.

Preoccupied with her and his own feelings, Doug drove the few blocks to the little house he rented. He did not think deeply into the questions she had raised about the missing records or seeming lies, because he well enough understood the clannish, suspicious nature of the people of Noble. It was simply one more manifestation of their kind of hate, he told himself. It meant nothing more. He was much more concerned with that moment that had passed between them and what might have happened. He wondered why he had let it pass—what both of them, perhaps in different ways, had been afraid of.

Because of his preoccupation, Doug Bennett did not see the black Ford cruise quietly down his street moments after he had gone inside. The car was parked and the engine shut off. The lone occupant remained behind the wheel, watching. Long after the lights had gone out in Doug's house, the shadowy figure remained in the car, watching, moving now and then as a pint bottle was raised, sipped from and put back on the seat.

CHAPTER 4

With her car packed before eight the next morning, Ruth gave the motel room a last glance to make sure she was leaving nothing behind. It looked even shabbier in the daylight, with the sagging bed unmade and rumpled from her restless night. She was glad to leave it.

At the motel office she paid the woman behind the counter.

"Planning to drive on now?" the woman asked. She wore a tentlike blue wrapper and furry slippers, and her hair was in big pink plastic curlers.

"I'll be here a little while yet," Ruth said.

The woman looked at her and seemed to make some decision. "I've heard you're looking into the Bartelson family."

"Oh?" Ruth murmured. She wondered how the woman had "heard" and how much other gossip was filtering through the little town. She felt a flush of irritation.

"Yes," the woman said, unaware. "You know, dear, if you want to talk to someone who knew Press Bartelson well, you really ought to go see my brother."

Ruth's curiosity rose. "He knew Press?"

"I should say so," the woman beamed. "They played on a championship football team together. I guess my brother Paul knew Press about as well as anybody ever did."

"Do you suppose he would talk about him?"

"I don't know why he wouldn't, dear. His name is Paul Buckingham and he handles real estate. His office is on Main Street about three doors from the hardware store. You can't miss it; it has pictures of houses in the front window. I was telling Paul on the phone last night that I had heard you were interested in the Bartelsons, and he said, 'Well, she should talk to me. I could tell her everything she wants to know,' and I said, 'Well, I'll mention it to her maybe, because she's a real nice person, seems like, and it would be a shame for her to miss out on some information when she's got a limited time in Noble.' And he said he would be glad to talk to you if you want. Well, I'm passing the word along, if you want more dope. We don't have a lot of out-of-town people except fishermen, and I guess some people here are sort of tight-mouthed, but my brother Paul isn't like that. He's a real friendly person—everyone says that. So you just feel free to go see him if you want, dear. I'm sure it would be his pleasure. He's a very genuine person."

Ruth said nothing for an instant, watching the woman's fat hands twist together, unclasp, twist again on the countertop. It had been a long speech, rehearsed. Why? Was there *fear* in the woman's eyes?

"I think I may just go see him," Ruth said aloud.

The heat was already back. A few high clouds, like burst brown sausages, obscured the sun now and then, but the humidity had gone very high. Locusts clattered in the trees. On Main Street, a few pickup trucks were parked here and there, and a semitrailer truck snorted through, leaving a thin haze of diesel fumes. Ruth had a remarkably good cup of coffee at the café and thought about Doug Bennett. Then she walked across the street to the narrow office entrance that had faded Polaroid photos of old-fashioned houses and farm buildings covering the front window.

The front office was icy cold from overworked air conditioning. Someone had plastered large calendars and fishing and hunting pictures clipped from magazines all over the high yellow plaster walls. The counter had a film of dust on it.

Paul Buckingham was short and rotund, and his seersucker jacket flapped open as he rushed out to the counter with a big grin and enveloped her hand in a clammy handshake. About fifty, or a little younger, he was growing out a crew cut with the result that cowlicks stuck up everywhere and hair bristled out around his ears. His eyes were close-set and bright with the effort of seeing around his prominent nose.

"I'm just *awfully* glad you stopped by!" he enthused, leading her into a doorway behind the counter that led to his private office. "So you want to find out everything about old Press Bartelson! Well, by golly, you came to the right place!"

Ruth took the brown plastic chair facing his littered desk. His office was paneled, some of the dark panels slightly askew as if it were a home-hobbyist job, and the two fluorescent fixtures suspended from the drop ceiling were too large. Two file cabinets stood in a corner. The chair Ruth was seated in was one of four lined along the outside wall. There were no windows, and on the paneling of one wall were a Rotary insignia, a framed Chamber of Commerce certificate, a paper from the Board of Realtors, a TWA calendar, a framed map of Noble that looked ancient, two little gold plaques, and a series of pictures of football teams, some posed in front of bleachers and others blurrily in action in a night game. It was the kind of wall one finds in small-town offices, where men measure out their lives remembering the only time that was ever good: high school, when hopes were strong and dreams could come true and girls were pretty.

Paul Buckingham, however, had learned to wear enthusiasm like his seersucker suit. Ruth briefly told him the reasons for her interest, omitting all reference to problems she had encountered, and the chubby salesman grinned broadly, ran his thick hand through the porcupine explosion of his hair and nodded delightedly.

"Say, that's fine!" he beamed at her. "And like I said, missy, you sure came to the right man. Like I was telling Dot—that's my sister—over at the house last night when she came by: I guess if I've got a favorite topic, it's old Press. He's about the biggest hero this old town ever had, you know."

"I didn't know." Ruth noticed but did not comment on the latest small lie. His sister had mentioned a telephone conversation; he had just mentioned a visit at his home. "Press was John Bartelson's only child?"

"Yessum, he sure was. The only child, but, golly, what a man he was! You know—"

"What happened to him, Mr. Buckingham?"

Buckingham frowned and leaned back in his swivel chair, trying again to slap down the porcupine quills around his ears. "Well, missy, that's the sixty-four-dollar question, I'd say. Or, like Dave Smith says down at the hardware, this is inflation, it's now a ninety-two dollar question but it's only worth about fourteen bucks." He waited and she gave him a dutiful smile.

"Well!" he went on with an explosive sigh. "Like I said, where's old Press today? I sure wish I knew, missy. I sure wish I knew. He left these parts in 1958. Went to Texas." His chair crying out from the sudden movement, he leaned forward and glared at some sheets of notepaper in the litter on his desk. "I got to thinking you might come by. I made some notes." He picked up some yellow notebook pages covered with red ballpoint scribbling. "Yep, here it is. I looked it up. Press left in July 1958. Went to Texas. He said he was going to Houston. Boom town, Houston. Have you ever been there?"

"No," Ruth murmured, making notes on her knee.

"Well, you'd be amazed. You'd be absolutely flabbergasted. *Really* a boom town. Not a town any more, of course; it's a big city by *anybody's* standards. Of course they've got the space thing there and the Astrodome and all. Hard to believe how that city has grown. Well, that's where old Press headed for in 1958. I guess he saw that was where the future was. He told us he was going to hook on with an oil company. Lots of oil around Houston, of course. He said he'd write, come back to visit. But he never has." Buckingham grinned and shook his head. "That's just *like* that old rascal!"

"Did he have a family?" Ruth asked. She felt impatience with Buckingham's folksy side excursions, and for reasons she did not fully understand she neither liked nor trusted him. But she told herself that most of this, at least, was probably very close to the truth. She was determined to learn all he would tell her.

"Family?" Buckingham echoed. "Well, no, missy, not really. His father, you know, died in '35, killed himself. That was a tragedy. A real tragedy. Depression got his business. He just never recovered. Right at the time when old Press was being All-State and our team was winning the state, old John Bartelson was drinking, going downhill." Buckingham sighed heavily. "Real tragic thing."

"How about Press's mother?"

"His mother?" Buckingham's eyes avoided hers for an instant, then came back. His hand patted his hair again. "Well, she died a little later, I'm sorry to say. I figured you'd want that, so I checked back in my files. I helped settle the house deal after she was gone. It was in 1947 she died. May 1947. I sold the house in August. It was a pretty nice house. It burned later, though. Struck by lightning, by golly. Just a vacant lot there now. It's over on Locust."

Ruth made notes. Then she looked up at Buckingham. "Is there anything more you can tell me about John Bartelson?"

Buckingham appeared surprised for an instant. "Old John? Well, not very much, missy. He was a good old boy. Everybody liked him. He stayed to himself a lot, though. Believed in me minding my business, him minding his. His store was nice before the Depression. He was on the school board once. I think he was undersheriff for a while, too."

Ruth nodded, thinking it wouldn't hurt to show she had *some* information, anyway. "Yes. That was in 1926."

Buckingham nodded and rocked in the chair. "Yep, I guess that would be about right. I was a kid then. Don't remember much about it. But I know the old man was pretty big, stout. Not fat, but stout, well built. He could handle himself. Wonderful shooter. Golly, I think he was champion skeet shooter or something once—did you know about that?"

"Yes."

Buckingham nodded. "Hmm."

There was nothing more about John. "Tell me about Press," Ruth urged.

Buckingham's grin came back. "Well, by golly, that's a pleasure! This was one great guy, missy, I'm here to tell you! He was built like his dad a lot, stocky, tough—but could he ever *run!* He started out as the starting fullback for the Broncos in the ninth grade! By the next year—I was a scrub guard that year—he was all-conference. He scored something like ten touchdowns and only a tenth-grader! *Run?* Say, you never *saw* anybody run with a football like old Press did. Inside. Outside. He had speed like you couldn't believe. And once we played Wewoka—they were ten times a bigger school than we *ever* were—in the mud up there at Wewoka, and old Press carried the ball something like fifty times, right up the middle, wham! bam! they couldn't hold him down, he scored three touchdowns in that mud and gained over two hundred yards and we won it, nineteen to twelve. That was when people started paying attention to us. We were coming. We had a good team that year—that was in '31. But in '32 we just killed everybody—why, you never saw anything *like* our team that year. It was unreal! I was starting guard that year and the next. I pulled, led the blocking outside for old Press, and Press was—well, he was just unreal. If you missed your block, he just gave the tackler a leg, and then took it back, and zip! he was gone! Or he just ran over people! We had a little dago quarterback named Shebara, he was great, too, and the combination, well, nobody knew how to stop us. That's all there is to it. Nobody knew how to stop us! We went to the state finals and Press got hurt and we lost, six-nothing. But then in '33 he was captain of the team and he was greater than ever." Buckingham stopped and picked up an old high-school annual off the desk. "Let me tell you some of the things he did."

He flipped pages, his aging face suffused with youthful joy. "Ah, here we go, here it is. Listen to this. 'Press Bartelson, number forty, starting fullback in the Broncos' terrific single wing attack. Press Bartelson stands six feet tall and weighs a hundred and ninety pounds. He can run the hundred in under ten seconds in his uniform. In this, his senior year, he led the Broncos to an undefeated season and the state Class C championship, defeating Eufaula for the title last December, twenty-six to six.' "

Buckingham grinned at Ruth and then continued reading.

" 'Press Bartelson has been called the greatest prep athlete in the history of Oklahoma. In his senior year, he rushed the ball two hundred and eighty-eight times, averaging twenty-four carries a game, and gained two thousand, three hundred and five yards'— did you get that? *Two thousand, three hundred and five yards*— 'for an average of eight yards per carry off the Broncos' buck-lateral system. Seven times in the twelve-game schedule, including playoff games, Press exceeded two hundred yards rushing in a single game, and his greatest night came in the championship game with Eufaula when he stormed for three hundred and nineteen yards'—did you get that? *Three hundred and nineteen* —'and all four of the Bronco touchdowns. He scored twenty-eight touchdowns this season. In addition, he punted eleven times for a forty-one-yard average and led the Broncos in tackles from his position as safety man.' "

Buckingham paused, closed the book and sighed. His pudgy fingers smoothed over the worn cover of the book with loving care. "He was," he said softly, his eyes on another time, "unreal."

Ruth knew that this part, at least, was authentic. "I'd give a lot to have a copy of that information for my uncle."

"Say, that's no problem! They've got a copying machine over at city hall, and I'll run over there after while and Xerox off a copy of these pages, if you like."

"I would appreciate that very much."

Buckingham patted at his hair again and sprang out of the chair. He pointed to one of the fading pictures framed on the paneled wall. "Like to see a picture of that championship team?"

Ruth stood and moved over to look at the yellowed eight-by-ten photograph in the small black frame. It showed the football team, in their helmets and uniforms that now looked quaintly old-fashioned, seated on the steps of bleachers. The players' faces stared out at the camera through a slight general blur.

"Here's old Press," Buckingham said reverently, touching his finger to the glass and leaving an oval oil mark. "And here's me. Right next to him. We were great buddies."

Ruth leaned close to peer at the faded, youthful face she could hardly recognize as Buckingham's. He had been slender then,

and he sat holding his helmet on his knee with a grim determina-
tion, a boy sure he would conquer the world.

She turned to Press Bartelson's photograph and felt a tingle
of recognition. He looked startlingly like Uncle Carl: the same
wide-set eyes, the same tawny hair, the same lean jaw line. The
eyes were dead into the camera and seemed to stare directly at
her out of the old photograph: eyes of a boy who was happy,
confident, solemn in his concentration.

"He was handsome," she observed.

"The girls adored him." Buckingham grinned, going back to
the desk. "Say, I guess everybody in Archer County adored him,
for that matter. But he was the nicest, humblest person you could
ever meet. Everybody loved him. Golly, he was the greatest thing
that ever *did* happen to the town of Noble!"

"Did he go to college?"

"Well, he tried it for a little while. He went to A and M, up at
Stillwater. But old Press was never much of one for the books. I
guess he just couldn't make it in the classes. He was the star of
their freshman team, but then he came back, said he had had
enough. People hated it; they'd *known* he would be all-American
up there and put Noble on the map. But you couldn't hold anything against old Press; he was just too dad-blamed lovable and
sweet and modest. He said he had had enough, and, by golly,
that was *it*. He opened him a sporting-goods store, did real fine.
Then he was just getting started, you know, and his dad killed
himself that way. That hurt Press a lot. I remember us talking
about it. He was never quite the same, even though he stayed on
for a long time. Then, like I told you, he went to Houston and
we lost track of him. I think sometimes he'll come back, and it'll
be a great reunion, I'll tell you for sure. Several of us who were on
that great team still live here. We still talk about it, some. Golly!"

"Press never married?"

"No, he never did. Too shy, I guess. He could have had his
pick of the girls."

Ruth hesitated, staring at her notes. But she was not reading
them. She was weighing alternatives. She sensed that this had
been the truth, at least most of it. There were enthusiasms, de-

tails, that couldn't be counterfeited. She struggled with the temptation to ask the final question, and then, on impulse, gave in to it.

"Mr. Buckingham," she said firmly, "why did some people lie about Press Bartelson?"

Buckingham's eyes bulged slightly. "Lie?"

"I might have come here and gone, not even knowing Press ever existed. I was even told that John Bartelson never married. *Why?* Do you have any idea? Can you tell me? It's the last thing, I guess, I really would like to know."

Buckingham's round jaw set and he turned and stared at the old pictures, the windows into the world where he still lived. For a long moment he said nothing, and Ruth could hear the chugging somewhere of the air-conditioning unit.

Then Buckingham sighed and faced her. "Well, I can tell you this. A town like Noble has one hero in a long, long time. There's not a lot left around here, you know. It's a good town. We all get by. But you *need* your heroes. You know?"

"But you haven't told me anything that shouldn't be known. I would expect people to be eager to tell about Press!"

Buckingham sighed again, and his eyes darted into a corner. "Well, there was a problem."

He paused, and Ruth said nothing, waiting. Her pulse whispered.

Buckingham looked at her almost defiantly. "I'm not going to tell you all the details. Nobody is. That's what everyone was hoping to hide, I guess. You never know, an outsider comes in, and, golly, maybe all they want is *dirt*—find one little problem, write something up that tears down everything Press stood for—everything he was."

"What happened?" Ruth asked simply.

Buckingham cocked his head and patted his hair again. "Well, missy, like I say," and his voice had a sudden, new, hard tone underlying it, "I won't give you a lot of lurid details. But there was a girl. She was common. To be frank with you, she was just a slut. Well, she said she was pregnant and Press was the father. Now I *know* that wasn't true! Press—why, he could have had the pick of *any* of the girls and a lot of the married women in town,

43

too, I bet, if you get right down to it. But he was modest and shy, a quiet person. I *know* he had nothing to do with that slut.

"But she was threatening to file suit, all that. So Press decided, well, the best thing was to pay her off. So we talked about it, and that was what he did, and she left. And that was when he went to Houston."

"And people didn't want an outsider to learn about that?"

"Press Bartelson was the greatest thing ever in Noble."

Ruth looked at Buckingham. He was being very careful to meet her gaze. For the first time since early in the interview she was aware of tension. Buckingham was feeling pressure and she didn't understand why. It was near the ugly fear she had sensed in his sister at the motel. *Why?*

"I'll respect your wishes," she told Buckingham. "There's no need to record anything about the problem with the girl."

Buckingham nodded with obvious relief and walked with her to the front door. There, standing in the empty-looking reception area, he held out his hand with a big smile. "I hope I've helped you out."

"You have. And I thank you for it."

"The thing about Press and the girl—well, that's confidential, as they say. Press was our hero here, you know. He still is."

"I understand," Ruth assured him.

Buckingham held the door for her, and the intense heat, heavy with humidity, gushed around them. The sky overhead was grayer now, the clouds coming down, pressing toward the earth.

"What will you do now?" Buckingham asked. "Be on your way?"

"Yes," Ruth said. "I plan to drive to the cemetery and take a picture of John Bartelson's grave, and then I'll come back, if I may, to pick up that copy from the high-school yearbook. And then I'll be going."

Buckingham's face wrinkled with a grin. "I'll sure have it for you then, missy!"

Thanking him once more, she crossed the street to her car, started it and turned on the air conditioning. The interior of the Vega was a humid furnace. She had consulted the county map

44

earlier and knew how to get to the cemetery, which was not far out of town to the south. She pulled out of the parking space and started away. In the doorway of the office, Buckingham sent her a broad grin, waved and tried again to slick down his hair.

Ruth turned past the city building, bounced across an old set of double railroad tracks, passed some shanty-quality housing and was headed out of Noble on a road narrowing to two crumbling blacktop lanes. As the Vega whisked down the first of a series of twisting hill curves, she wondered why there had been the lie about how Buckingham and his sister had spoken of her. The story of Press's involvement with a girl, too, did not ring quite true to her; there had been that slight evasive look in Buckingham's eyes at that point.

She had much more of the story, she thought. She believed all of it about Press Bartelson and football and the town's adoration. But now Press was gone, and the town brooded about some secret, and she was not at all sure she was any closer to what that secret really might be. She wondered if she really wanted to know. She thought of Doug Bennett again and wished he were here.

McAlester was awake under a brooding sky when Doug Bennett drove in with the librarian from the town of Harvert a little before nine o'clock. He had left Noble at seven, driven the back road to Harvert, picked up Bryce Kinsolving a little before eight and cut over to the Interstate Highway to make better time.

"Right on the money," said Kinsolving, a bald little man of sixty, as they drove into the downtown area. Kinsolving had spent his life in southeastern Oklahoma, liked it, was happy in the tiny Harvert library, and had regaled Doug with stories of user problems on the way. "I'd hate to be late for one of these scintillating meetings, wouldn't you?"

Doug braked his car for a traffic signal that turned red as he approached. He was second in line behind a new Buick, and a recent-model Pontiac pulled up beside him on his left as he waited. "I hope they have doughnuts," he said.

"Your attitude," Kinsolving sighed, "is execrable." He gestured

around the square at the great old business buildings, the ginger-
bread hotel and line of stores with false fronts and movie theater
that advertised *Around the World in Eighty Days* on its marquee.
"Consider the cultural benefit of visiting the city!"

"It does look like a city to me this time," Doug admitted.
"Which may be part of my problem."

The light changed. The Buick moved off. Doug pressed on the
accelerator. His car engine labored and then seemed to spin free.
Underneath, the transmission made a howling noise. The car
barely limped off from a halt.

"Problems?" Kinsolving said worriedly.

Doug checked the gear selector and glanced at the panel, which
told him nothing, any informative instruments having been re-
placed by flasher lights. "I don't know," he muttered. He fed the
car more gas, but it continued to shudder, hardly moving.

The farm truck behind him moved out and around, accelerating in a faint cloud of oil smoke. The fat driver shot him a dirty
look.

"Something is sick in the transmission," Doug decided. "The
engine's fine. I'm just not getting any connection with the
wheels."

"Garage just around that next corner," Kinsolving pointed out.

Disgusted, Doug nodded and virtually coasted the car around
the corner on a red light, then limped into the driveway. The
front door of the Ford garage was open. His momentum carried
him part way in. He tried to move up, but the car sat there, refusing to move. Smoke issued from underneath.

The chief mechanic came over with a clipboard. He looked
cheerful and observed that Doug seemed to have a problem.
Kinsolving got out and shook hands with him; they were old
friends. The mechanic turned back to Doug with a slightly
more concerned attitude. He suggested leaving the car—which
was good, since Doug had no choice—and going on to the meeting. He said he would assign the transmission man to look into it
immediately. Could Doug call back in an hour? The mechanic
said that would be fine and dandy.

46

"Well," Kinsolving sighed as they walked the few blocks toward the library, "maybe it won't be serious."

"Maybe not," Doug grunted, mystified and irritated. "I just had the regular checkup on the damned thing and changed the transmission fluid. I thought it was in perfect shape."

"Well, it broke down at a good time."

Doug lit a cigarette and said nothing. He felt bitter disappointment. There, he thought, probably went his last chance of getting back in time, before she left this afternoon.

"I had transmission trouble in the Rambler a year ago," Kinsolving volunteered. "Gosh. It cost three hundred and forty-two dollars before they had it right again."

They reached the library a few minutes late, but the meeting started even later, as usual. Opening remarks and a report took about thirty minutes, and then there was a coffee break. The mimeographed agenda called for a presentation by a man from the state library board at ten. Doug, carrying a soggy doughnut with him, went into an office and called the garage.

"I know I'm a little early," he told the chief mechanic when he came on the line, "but I might be tied up for a while. Any word yet on my car?"

The mechanic spoke over the distant sound of rivet guns and other equipment echoing in the garage. "I'm afraid you've got a real problem there. Going to have to take it completely down."

"How long will *that* take? And how much?"

"Well, we can't know until we get into it, of course. But Bill says it looks to him like the whole main assembly is gummed up, your converter is entirely gone—I'd say we'll be lucky to get it out today. I'll have him start on it right away, but it might be noon tomorrow. Probably cost in the neighborhood of two hundred."

"Christ. I just had that thing checked and the fluid changed less than a month ago!"

"You what?"

Doug repeated it.

There was a silence on the other end.

"Are you there?" Doug asked.

"I wouldn't say this," the mechanic told him finally, "but you're a friend of old Bryce's, and a man ought to know. If you had that transmission checked and the fluid changed recently, then I'd say you ought to check where you're parking your car. Either you've got some vandalism or you've got an enemy around."

Doug tensed. "What do you mean by that?"

"Well, sir, Bill told me he never seen a transmission any dirtier."

"That's impossible!"

"Bill showed me some of the gluk he drained out of it. There wasn't much left inside. It heated up and your front seal went. But I'd have to agree with Bill. I never saw any nastier, glukkier stuff in my life. Man, you had tar and dirt and sand and everything else in there. It just flat tore the transmission to pieces. I'd say, just guessing, you understand, that somebody dumped that crap in there on you with *the intent* of wrecking your car for you."

Doug stood very still, holding the telephone to his ear.

"Hello?" the mechanic said after a long pause.

Doug had been thinking. "When would it have happened?"

"Are you from Harvert, like Bryce?"

"No. Noble."

"Noble, down in Archer County?"

"Yes."

"Well, buddy, if you got all the way from Noble today, I'd say your car is hell for stout. I don't know how you got that far in it. It must have just been did. You must've come on the throughway and your transmission didn't have to shift much. I sure hate to tell a man bad news, but it's a miracle you made it this far. Somebody must have done this last night."

"I see. Okay. Thanks."

"Should we start work on it?"

"Yes. Right away."

He left the small cubicle office and walked back down the hall to the meeting room. The other librarians, most of them women, stood around the paneled room with their coffee cups. Doug tried to come to terms with the thoughts tumbling through his brain.

48

Only one theory made any sense, he decided. He was angry and mixed up.

"What did they have to say?" Kinsolving grinned as Doug walked up to join him and two women standing near the coffee urn.

"I'm afraid it's serious," Doug told him.

"Say, I'm sorry to hear that. Will they have it fixed by noon?"

"No way. Look, Bryce. Could you get a ride back to Harvert with someone else?"

"Well, I suppose so. Maybe Jennings will be going that way, or Madge—"

"Okay. Get any releases or materials they pass out, will you?"

"Where are *you* going?"

"Something has come up," Doug told him. "I'm going to find a rental car. I have to get right back to Noble."

CHAPTER 5

The cemetery was scattered over the side of a hill. The newer section, nearer the dirt road where Ruth had parked the car, was surrounded by a waist-high stone fence, and the pink and white marble markers stood well apart in grassy plots that showed some evidence of care. The older section, shading into old slabs amid weeds near the top of the hill, was fenced by black pipes set in rotting fenceposts. The sky overhead churned, dark and heavy with turbulent rain likely to begin at any time. The hot wind whipped elms and gnarled oaks and bent slender evergreens in the newer section.

The dry grass tugging at her ankles, Ruth moved systematically from grave to grave part way up the hill. She was in the transitional area, some of the stones fairly new, others old, weathered, a few fallen over and untended. The wind pressed her hair over her face and she brushed it back irritably, holding her camera. She was beginning to wonder if she could find it alone.

Coming to the end of a row of stones, she was about to walk to the next, higher up, when she spotted the low double marker partially obscured by weeds. It was near a tall cottonwood, bending and sighing in the wind. A few pale-blue wildflowers poked up out of the high grass, and an old metal vase that had once held cut flowers stood at a crazy angle to one side in its rusting lattice retainer.

The low, three-foot gray marker had a slanted face, which was the only reason she spotted the single word in big letters centered across the top: BARTELSON.

Squatting beside the marker, Ruth pressed the weeds back from the lower portion of the stone. The left side read:

JOHN A.
1890–1935

So here they were.

Pleased with herself for having found it, Ruth slowly stood and moved around, seeking the best angle for her photograph. She decided first to back off and take a long shot. Through her viewfinder she framed the marker in the lower left corner, with the trunk of the cottonwood and some of the other stones in the line angling back to the right. She read the exposure carefully and pressed the shutter release, then moved to her right to take another shot with the marker centered in the finder.

Moving in, she focused again and saw that the weeds partially obscured the words and dates on the side she had just read and wholly covered the right side of the stone. She took one shot this way, and then knelt beside the stone to press down the weeds and high grass. It was so dry that many blades broke off, clearing the engraved letters. She pressed the grass well down on both sides of the stone, then got back to her feet, moved a few feet away, cocked her camera and focused again.

As she pressed the shutter, she read—for the first time—the lettering on the right-hand side of the marker. The meaning of the letters registered only as the shutter flicked open and closed.

Feeling electric surprise, she lowered the camera and stared at the marker to assure herself that her vision was correct. She read the entire marker again, and as she did so the implications of her surprise continued to seep into her, like cold sludge.

The marker read:

BARTELSON
JOHN A.	GLADYS S.
1890–1935	*1895–*

She continued to stare at it, aware of the wind in the big trees and the high hum of the force of air through the clouds overhead, the rolling, desolate, wooded countryside beyond the confines of the little cemetery.

Why?

The sound of a car's tires on gravel came distantly. She turned, startled.

A black sedan had pulled in behind the Vega on the road at the foot of the hill. The front door of the sedan opened and Chuck Vachon ponderously got out. He wore a yellow sports shirt and gray slacks and a broad-brimmed Western-style hat. Holding the brim of the hat against the rising humid wind, he peered at her car for a moment, then slowly turned his head to look up the hill. She saw his body stiffen slightly as he spied her.

She started down the hill through the graves. Seeing her approaching, Vachon stood beside his car, one booted foot hiked up on a stone in the wall.

A little out of breath, she walked down the hillside, through the gate and past her car to where he stood. His eyes, slitted against the wind, studied her carefully although there was the ritualistic grin on his mouth.

"Well, howdy do," he said. "I saw the car and needed to make sure it hadn't been stolen."

"Really?" Ruth snapped. "Is this road part of your regular beat?"

Vachon's beefy face wrinkled as the smile died. "What's the trouble? Couldn't you find whatever you were looking for?"

"Is that any of your business? Or perhaps it is. You seem to think quite a lot is your business. Tell me, Mr. Vachon, what made you think my car had been stolen?"

"Well, I swan," Vachon murmured. "You're really upset about *something*, I see. But there's no need to light into *me*. I'm just doin' my job the best way I know how."

"Just as you were last night when you followed me to the library?" Ruth shot back, knowing she was being reckless but momentarily beyond caring.

Vachon frowned again. "What's got into you?"

"I'll tell you. People in this town have lied to me since the moment I drove in yesterday. Last night it *might* have been an accident that you showed up back at the library when I returned there. But I don't think so now. Not after you *just happened* to appear out here too. Why are you following me?"

Vachon's heavy face creased more deeply, and under puffy lids his eyes became opaque—ugly with the gray of oil on water. "It's my job to watch out for people."

"Why should you have to look after me? I can take care of myself."

"You don't know people around here. A lot of 'em distrust strangers—"

"Is that why they're so good at lying?"

"You keep sayin' that. What are you hintin'?"

"I'm not *hinting*, Mr. Vachon. I was told lies when I asked about John Bartelson. I was told lies when I asked about his family. Now I come out here and learn it was even a lie when I was told Gladys Bartelson is dead!"

"What do you mean by that? Of course she's dead!"

"Her tombstone is right up there," Ruth retorted, pointing. "Would you like to examine it yourself? There's no date of death on it!"

Vachon smiled unconvincingly. "Izzat all? Well, I swan. Don't you know they can forget to carve in dates sometimes? Heck fire. I know that old lady died long ago! She was real poor, there wasn't any survivors, maybe nobody paid to have her date carved in on the thing."

The theory was just possible enough to make Ruth hesitate. "I might have believed that yesterday," she said, still angry. "Now I don't know."

"Are you callin' me a liar?"

"I'm saying I don't know who to believe around here! And I don't appreciate your following me!"

Vachon's fists balled, and suddenly she was aware that he could be a dangerous man, one capable of many things. His eyes were smoke-filled. "People have been real nice to you," he told her. "Don't push your luck."

"Don't tell *me* not to push my luck!" Ruth replied, the full force of her rage carrying her beyond caution again. "I came here to ask a few simple questions about an old man. I could have been told the truth—whatever the truth is—in about ten minutes. All I've gotten is evasion or worse. I—"

Vachon reached out and caught her arm. The force of his grip shocked her as he jerked her close. He held her helpless, like a doll, and his breath was warm and sickly sweet with whiskey.

"Now let me tell you a thing or two," he grunted.

"Let go of me!"

"This is *our* country," he grated, continuing to hold her helpless. "You don't belong here, you know that? You've got no right, comin' in here with your fancy talk and fancy clothes and snotty manners, pushin' people around. I been real patient with you. I've just about had it. Now I'm *tellin'* you: You finish up your business in Noble quick, an' you git *out* of here!"

With that, he released his hold and shoved her back. She staggered against the rear fender of the Vega, nearly falling. Her breath caught in her throat and she held her numbed arm and stared at him, the fear thick inside and making her weak.

Vachon pointed a trembling hand at her. "I mean it."

An angry reply was on her lips, but Ruth held it back. She turned. Her vision was blurry with hot tears. She opened the car door and flung herself inside, tossing the camera on the front seat beside her. She started the engine and turned the car sharply, scattering gravel on the narrow roadway. She had to back around. Vachon stood beside his cruiser, hands on hips, watching her. She completed her maneuver and floored the accelerator, the rear wheels spinning and throwing more gravel as she headed back up the hill toward town.

Reaching the top, she glanced in the rear-view mirror. The black sedan had turned around and was following her.

The first moments of the confrontation behind her, she felt weak, her legs and arms almost without strength. Cool sweat filmed her body. Shakily she fumbled in her purse for cigarettes as she maintained a sharp pace on the curving, hilly road.

Anger was vying with the fear. She had known this mixture of feelings only one time before, the night a youth tried to take her purse in the parking lot of the apartment complex back home. That time she had reacted instinctively, and the guard had been there in seconds in answer to her scream. She had run the gamut in those first moments then: outrage that someone would attack her, try to take something from *her,* because when it happened to oneself it was sharp and fresh and different from all the remote accounts in the newspapers; and then she had gone weak as the fear reaction set in.

It was like that now. She struggled to get herself back together, drawing deeply on the cigarette, glancing in the rear-view mirror, seeing the sedan briefly as it topped a rise behind her. She was bitterly angry that Vachon had—had *hurt* her this way, and threatened her. But there was a sharp, weakening sense of relief, too.

It could have been worse.

The amazing thing was that she still didn't know why. Had she made a serious blunder, telling him what she had found? More important, *was* John Bartelson's widow still alive?

She needed help now. She needed help badly. For the first time she was frightened. All she wanted to do was go back, get the page copies from Paul Buckingham at the real-estate office and leave. She told herself she had enough information. And yet another part of her struggled against this impulse. She would *not* be frightened away, that part of her said.

She reached the blacktop road and turned onto it, accelerating again. She drove recklessly. A few spatters of rain made big pink mud splotches on the windshield and then ceased. The wind rocked the trees.

Vachon's sedan trailed her the rest of the way into Noble and went slowly past as she parked again in front of the real-estate office. She fought to maintain her composure as she went inside. Buckingham had the copies and bestowed them upon her as if they were precious.

Thanking him, she left the office.

"Guess you'll be leaving now, eh, missy?" Buckingham grinned from the door.

It struck her forcefully that Buckingham, too, was eager to get rid of her. She was baffled. She remembered her childhood, how her mother had scolded her: "You're too stubborn for your own good! The world won't change just because you throw a tantrum, Miss Priss!"

Was she being a fool now, childish because she wasn't getting her way? She told Buckingham, "I'll be going very shortly, yes. Thanks again."

Buckingham waved and went back into his vacant office.

Putting the copies on the front seat of her car, she looked toward the city building. Only two official slots in front were occupied. One was a green Ford, the other the black car that Vachon had evidently driven around the block and parked. He was not in sight. Doug Bennett's car was not there, and she could see that the parking places on the side street were empty.

Doug, I need you, she thought.

Pulling the car around in the street, she turned and parked in front of the drugstore. Two housewives left the store carrying small sacks and looking apprehensively toward the sky. The wind drove small clouds of dirt along the broken slabs of pavement, and the metal sign over the doorway swayed back and forth, creaking on its holders.

Ruth ran into the drugstore. A couple of high-school-age boys were at the soda fountain counter, having Cokes. Alvin Crewser, calm and cool as usual, gave her a smile as she forced the door closed against the wind.

"Hello again!" he said. "I thought you had gone by now."

Catching her breath, Ruth gave him a smile in return and headed for the fountain counter. "Just finishing up."

Crewser came out from behind the cigars and patent medicines and followed her, moving in behind the fountain. "Can I get you something? I'm a little short-handed today, handling it alone this morning."

"Coffee," Ruth said.

Crewser drew a cup and placed it before her. "Like anything else?"

"No. Thank you."

"Certainly going to have a big storm," Crewser said, looking toward the dust-filled street beyond the windows.

Ruth said nothing. Her hands trembled as she manipulated the cup.

"So you found out everything you needed to know," Crewser said.

"Yes," she said huskily. She needed to steady herself and decide her next move. If there was to be another move. It might be better just to get into the car and get on the road.

"Well," Crewser sighed, "it's too bad you'll be driving through rain, but I guess we can certainly use it. No doubt about that. We've had a dry summer. Far below average."

Thinking about it, Ruth came up with two long-shot possibilities. "I do have a telephone call to make, Mr. Crewser. Do you have a telephone?"

"Sure do. Booth's in the back there."

"Save my coffee?"

"Why, sure."

Clutching her purse, she went back between the musty counters to the ancient brown metal booth beside the magazine rack. The telephone directory was the size of a small magazine. She made it a point to look for herself, was not surprised when there was no "Bartelson" listed. Then she turned to the yellow pages. She found the number she sought.

The telephone had no dial. She dropped the dime and waited.

"Number please?" the operator said in a Southwestern twang.

"Seven eight seven four," Ruth said.

There was a slight pause. Then the woman told her, "The library is closed this morning."

"Will you ring the number anyway?"

"But the library is closed."

"Just ring the number. *Please.*"

"All right." The operator sounded indignant.

There was some scratching and clicking, and then the sound

of the telephone whirring its ring. Ruth waited. It rang seven
times, eight, nine. Ruth stood in the brown metal booth, watching
the two high-school boys at the counter shove at each other and
spill one of their Cokes. Please answer, she thought. It was impossible, but—

"Hello?"

"Doug?" She could hardly believe it.

"Yes. Is this—"

"Ruth Baxter. I didn't think you'd be back! Doug, listen—"

"I just walked in the door and the phone was ringing," he
told her. "I came back in a pickup truck that belongs to a garage
in McAlester. I was trying to figure out how I could locate you
if you were still in town."

"I'm at the drugstore."

"I'm coming right over." The connection broke.

She left the booth and walked back to the counter. The two
boys had gone, and Crewser was mopping up their mess. "Get
your party?" he asked cheerfully.

"Yes."

"Warmed your coffee for you."

Ruth glanced toward the vacant red leatherette booths behind
the racks. "I'm going to take it to a booth, Mr. Crewser, and
could you bring another cup, please? Someone is joining me."

Crewser's eyes were sharp for an instant before he guarded
them. "That right? Well, fine."

Going to the booth with her cup, she took the side that allowed
her to face toward the door. The booths were so imbedded in
racks of medicines and goods that she had only a partial view.
The wind was even higher, sending gusts of dirt that made the
view across the street obscure from time to time.

She waited impatiently, sipping her coffee. Alvin Crewser
brought another cup of the steaming stuff and set it down facing
her. "One last interview?" he asked.

"Yes."

He stood by the table a moment. He wanted more information.

She said nothing. She felt defiant.

Crewser left, walked behind the fountain, rearranged a few dishes and swiped the counter with a towel again, then went across the store to the cigar counter. He stood behind the counter impassively, watching the dust fly outside.

Ruth continued to feel strong impatience. The knowledge that Doug Bennett was in town, and coming to her, made things seem considerably brighter. She realized that she had already begun to think of him as a friend. It had been a long time since she had instinctively felt close to someone in this way. There were things about him she didn't understand; he was not a simple person: his bitterness, when it surfaced, contradicted his basically quiet nature. She imagined there was strong feeling beneath that placid surface; the bitterness, when it broke through, was only one manifestation. The trip to Noble would be memorable for having met him, she thought, even if the other unusual aspects suddenly cleared up.

She was wondering if she would ever see him after she left today when the front door opened and he blew in. He glanced toward the back and she waved. He hurried back. His collar was open, his tie sideways.

"Don't ever try to drive a pickup with a winch on the back in this kind of gusty wind," he said, dropping to the bench opposite her at the table. "I pushed it all the way. I was afraid you'd be gone. I've had a little adventure." He paused and looked intently at her. "You're pale! What's happened?"

Ruth felt the tears really trying to let go and she was astonished. She was being very silly. "I'm just glad to see a friendly face."

Doug's eyebrows slanted together. "Something *has* happened. Tell me."

She told him about the visit with Paul Buckingham and then about the cemetery—and Chuck Vachon.

Doug's face was dark when she finished. "I wasn't really hurt, of course. Just frightened. And a little confused. I'm almost getting used to that—"

"The son of a bitch."

"It's all right. I'm fine."

"It's *not* all right!" He was bitterly angry. "Who told him he has that kind of authority? I've taken plenty from him since I've been back, but this is too much."

Ruth smiled. "Doug, it's *all right*." She was secretly pleased —and mystified by the pleasure—that he was so angry on her behalf. "I'm just fine, see?" She held up her arms. "Nothing broken."

"Not this time, anyway. What about the next? Your little family-tree research has stepped on some toes."

"You said *you* had an adventure. What did you mean?"

"Someone fooled with my car."

"You had a *wreck?*"

His smile was too grim to betray humor. "No, nothing like that. Not that original. They filled my transmission full of dirt, and it went out on me in McAlester."

"Why would someone—?"

"I've thought about that all the way back. I still come up with my first idea, which is why I got back here in a hurry." He paused and looked at her. "Somebody didn't want me to come back in time to see you again. They wanted to make sure you got no more help around here and got on your way as quickly as possible."

"So they wrecked your car transmission? That's a little hard to believe!"

"A lot of this is getting a little hard to believe."

"But if what you say is true, *why?* I've asked that question about a hundred times, and I still come up with zero!"

Doug drained his coffee cup in a swallow. "You say that stone made it appear the widow is still alive?"

"There was no date—"

"All right. I know a few people in this town. You sit tight. I'm going to make some phone calls."

As he started to get up, she reached out and caught his arm. He stopped dead, staring at her in surprise.

"Maybe we shouldn't," she said, feeling a sudden deep chill.

"Why?" he asked quietly.

"I don't know. I don't have to know any more. I can leave. Whatever happened—whatever someone wants to keep hidden

—maybe we should just let it alone. I don't want you hurt, and I've decided I might be a coward. Maybe we should stop."

Doug continued to look down at her. He took a deep breath. "If you say so," he replied finally, "that's the way it will be. For myself, I'm a little tired of being pushed around. I've tried just about my best to maintain a low profile in this town. But there's a limit. I've reached it."

"But you could still just forget the whole thing." She was not at all sure why she was arguing this way.

"Not now I couldn't," he told her. "I'm terribly old-fashioned, you see. I take it extremely personally when someone messes up my car or scares the daylights out of my girl."

"Your girl?" she repeated instantly, and then wished she hadn't.

His face flamed. "That was an idiot remark. I was thinking that—well, they must equate us that way. I'm sorry. It was stupid."

Her own nervous laugh surprised her. "I don't really mind your saying it." Then she heard her own words and was stunned. "I mean—I wasn't offended."

Their eyes met and held, and she felt her heart beat. She had been caught totally by surprise.

Doug seemed to recover first. He broke the gaze and leaned his hands on the tabletop. "Look," he said softly. "If you don't want me to make these calls, that's fine. I don't have to mount a vendetta over damage to a car."

She was still unsettled by their exchange. "I don't know what to say."

"Your choice," he said.

She saw what he was really saying: I'll help if you want me to, but I won't press you because neither of us knows what this is all about, or where it might lead us.

The uncertainty was not just about whatever mystery might be hidden. It also had to do with them and the feeling between them.

"Well?" Doug said quietly.

"Call," she said.

He nodded and headed back toward the telephone booth.

Ruth remained where she was, toying with her own empty coffee cup. She was in a quiet tumult. She felt above and beyond everything else that it was just too much, too fast: Vachon's threat, the question of the marker, Doug's return, the ruining of his car, his anger and offer of new help, what he had said about her being his "girl." The last was as startling as any of the other, especially in terms of her own reaction to it.

She had told herself that she had felt that kind of feeling for the last time, that it was something one felt once, if she was lucky, and then only when she was very young. She was not all that young now. She was, she reminded herself, twenty-seven years old. That felt very old indeed. She had heard all the lines and fended off all the passes, from the cocktail propositions to the oil-smooth maneuvers of men who considered themselves experts. A few of these approaches had irritated her, a couple had been amusing, but most had been simply boring, the same old try.

And now, after knowing this man less than a day, in just about the most impossible place she could have imagined, she felt quite differently. She felt numb because of it.

Her thoughts were interrupted at this point by Alvin Crewser. He was back at the booth with the coffee urn and had said something.

"What?" she replied, startled.

He grinned. "I said, more coffee?"

"Oh. Yes. Please."

He filled the cup. "More for Doug too, you suppose?"

"Yes," she said absent-mindedly.

He poured again. "Making a call for you, is he?"

She said nothing. He was prying again and she wished she knew why.

Crewser put the coffee urn on the edge of the table. "He's a good man, you know that? I like him. I think a lot of people like Doug Bennett. It takes a special kind of man to go through what he went through over there and then come back and work in a little town like this. I admire him for it."

He was making her nervous. She lit a cigarette and refused to answer him.

"You're lucky you hit it off with him," Crewser went on, still standing there with no intention of moving. "Whatever information you look for, I guess it's best if you find a librarian, right?"

"Right," she replied mechanically.

"You know," Crewser told her, "when you came in yesterday, I sort of wish I had been more helpful myself, now."

Ruth looked up at him, into the sincere grin. "You mean you didn't give me all the help you could, Mr. Crewser?"

"Ouch. I deserved that. Of course you know by now I didn't tell you all the truth, by any means."

"Do I?"

"I should have been more candid. I see that now. Could have saved you some trouble. But I guess maybe by now you can understand. You see, Press was awfully special around here. We try to . . . protect his image, if you know what I mean."

Ruth was pressed into genuine comment despite herself. With a trace of heat she replied, "I'm not interested in spoiling anyone's reputation, Mr. Crewser. I'm not here to ruin the image of the town hero. I simply came here to get some information for a family tree."

"I know, I know," Crewser sighed. He added meaningfully, "Now."

"You could have saved me a great deal of trouble and worry."

"I know that, too, and I'm sorry."

"Good. We can just forget about it."

"I guess so, because you do have the entire story now, don't you?"

Ruth looked up at him. She felt reckless again, pressed by all the lies and seeming good nature that had gone sour since her arrival in this town.

She said, "I imagine you know exactly what I've been told."

Crewser held his smile. "Please?"

"I said, I imagine—"

"Yes, I heard you, but I don't understand."

"I mean that I'm sure you've been informed by your friends along the street here—Mr. Buckingham and others—exactly what I've been told."

He was surprised but recovered well. "To some extent, yes.

We do talk. We're all old friends, you know. You learn to stick together in places like Noble."

"I'm learning that. Yes."

"But you have it all now, I'm sure."

"I'm not," Ruth said.

Crewser looked at her.

"Is Gladys Bartelson still alive?" she asked.

"Of course not!" Crewser said as if shocked.

"I see."

"Whatever gave you such an idea?"

"Nothing," she murmured, wishing Doug would hurry.

"She died long ago," Crewser insisted.

"All right."

Crewser stood there a moment. Then he said, "You have to forgive us our peculiarities, Miss Baxter. I know we seem strange to people such as you, from large cities. But here we tend to be private."

"I understand," Ruth said, tight-lipped.

Crewser picked up the coffee urn. Did he want to say something more? He took the coffee back to the fountain, then returned to his station by the front cash register.

Ruth sipped the coffee and waited some more. Several minutes passed. She could not see the telephone booth from where she waited. Outside, the wind seemed to slacken for a little while, then gust harder than ever. She heard it howling against the building and could taste the fine red dust beginning to make the inside of the drugstore seem faintly smoky.

She wondered how badly she had erred in letting both Vachon and Crewser know of her doubt about Gladys Bartelson. But given the little she knew, and the track record of information in this town, she felt she had every reason to be doubtful. She was not betraying a curiosity, she realized, that they might not guess anyhow once they knew she had seen the tombstone.

More minutes passed, and she was almost ready to walk back to see what was keeping Doug, when suddenly he strode back down the aisle.

"Your coffee is probably cold," she told him. "Did you—"

She stopped, then, as he reached for his wallet and took out a dollar bill, putting it on the table.

"Come on," he said sharply.

She did not question him. She rose instantly and followed him out of the store, past Crewser at the front counter, into the howling wind and humid heat beyond the doors.

She didn't know what Doug had learned, but he had learned something. His face told her that.

CHAPTER 6

Outside, the wind had again slacked off, but boiling black clouds seemed almost at the rooftops. Doug stopped outside the drugstore and glanced momentarily toward the city building, where a black and white winch truck—the one he had borrowed—was parked. Ruth thought he looked off-balance and worried.

"Doug? What is it?"

"Can we take your car?"

"Yes, but—"

"Good."

She followed him, and he went to the driver's side. She walked around to the far side of the Vega and got in as he slammed his door. She handed him the keys. He started the engine and backed out to head north, away from the downtown area.

There were few men she would have allowed to take over this way. She sensed it was no time to make an issue of it. "Where are we going?"

"Just a couple of blocks," he said, turning at the corner and heading west along the street that was the state route. They jounced over the railroad tracks.

"What did you find out?"

"Maybe a whole lot," he said. "Maybe not. But we can probably put it together pretty fast." He was pale.

"Is Gladys Bartelson alive?"

He looked at her briefly. "Yes."

66

She said nothing. She was not surprised.

Ahead was an intersection and a twist in the street. On one corner was an old warehouse, abandoned, and on another a decrepit gas station with several old cars parked at the side. Ruth wanted to question Doug but resisted. She was beginning to understand him. He didn't play games. He would tell her when he got his thoughts collected.

In a moment he said, "She's not only alive. She's still living here."

Before Ruth could ask anything more, he turned abruptly and wheeled the car into the ramp of the gas station. He didn't pull up beside the pumps but parked at the side. The station had once been white tile, but accumulated dust, grease and age had stained it a grayish brown. Empty oil barrels stood along the narrow walk leading to the side restrooms, and along with the abandoned old cars were tires, rims, fenders, bumpers, an entire engine rusting on the ground, a half acre of miscellaneous automotive junk extending back into the cover of weeds in the empty field behind. It crossed her mind that technology erected monuments to itself like this.

"I'm going in here a minute," Doug told her, opening the door.

"I'm coming too."

The front door of the glassed-in station was closed against the blowing dust. Doug held it for her and they went in. The office area was about ten feet square, with red-and-black shelving along the rear wall cluttered with flashlights, oil, lighters, decals, batteries, cheap Ozarks souvenirs. The glass counter cutting the tiny space in half was covered with old newspapers and more souvenir racks, and the cash register stood precariously on the window ledge in the middle of a display of STP cans. The floor was oily underfoot and the place smelled of tobacco and gasoline. A small, oil-smeared Arvin radio, once pink, blared country music from the top of the shelving.

The door to the garage area was open and a car was up on the rack. A heavy tool clanked onto metal somewhere and the owner of the station came in from that area, wiping grease from his big hands on a red industrial towel. He was tall, thickset, with tangled black hair cut short. He had thick lips of the kind sometimes described as cruel, and he wore filthy coveralls. He was probably in his late twenties, Ruth thought. The stub of a cigar was clamped in his teeth.

He gave Ruth a glance, then turned to Doug and swung out an open hand in stiff, almost formalized masculine greeting. "Hey, buddy. How's the car running?" He was rough-voiced, adding to Ruth's dominant impression that he was probably best here in a service station, with men, dressed roughly and manhandling heavy parts.

"Ted Spandecker," Doug told him, "I'd like you to meet Ruth Baxter. Mrs. Baxter is visiting in Noble."

Spandecker nodded to her with no trace of a smile. "You'd be the one checking into a family history deal," he said.

"Word gets around," she observed.

Spandecker shrugged. "Small town." He turned back to Doug. "What can I do for you?"

"Mrs. Baxter is interested in John Bartelson. She's also interested in Press."

Spandecker's lips set as he removed the gummy cigar stub and deposited it on the edge of the counter. "Never knew him."

"Your father did," Doug said.

"Did he?" There was a trace of challenge in Spandecker's tone.

"They belonged to the club together," Doug told him.

Spandecker tossed his grease rag onto the counter, picked up the stub of cigar again, inserted it between his teeth, took out an old Zippo lighter with a military insignia on the battered side, applied flame to the butt and looked at Doug through eyes slitted against the smoke. He said nothing.

"Do you know what happened to him?" Doug insisted quietly.

Spandecker leaned over an oil can in the corner and released a stream of spittle that splashed into fluid already in the bottom. "Accident," he grunted.

"I know that much."

Spandecker faced Doug and slowly folded brawny arms over his chest. "You won't hear any more from me, buddy." His whole attitude was quietly antagonistic.

68

Doug's face showed he did not like to rake over old wounds. But he was determined. "You don't know any details about the accident?"

Slowly Spandecker turned to the counter and picked up the grease rag. He wiped his hands again. His expression was flinty, and Ruth thought he might not reply at all.

"No details," he said finally. He took a deep breath and turned toward the garage door. "I've got a brake job I promised by noon, so—"

"It's not like a stranger was asking you," Doug said.

"It was a long time ago."

"I know. But it won't lie, will it?"

"It will," Spandecker snapped. "It has and it will. It's over. A long time ago."

"Is that the way you want it?" Doug countered.

Spandecker's face blotched with suppressed anger. "It ain't what I want that matters. It's what's got to *be*, buddy. I run a business here. I get along. You don't get along by raking over old coals."

"All I'm asking is exactly how it happened."

"And all I'm telling you is to forget it!"

Spandecker was openly angry. Ruth expected Doug to see it was useless to keep trying. But he was more stubborn than *she* was.

"Was it on the old state route?"

"I don't *talk* about it," Spandecker replied angrily. "I get along. You *understand*, buddy? I *get along*."

The two men faced each other, the strength of their wills clashing and falling back in the space between them. Doug was very angry now, and so was Spandecker, with a hushed, repressed frustration of some kind that Ruth could not fathom. She had felt this intense emotion in others in this town, but not so strongly. It frightened her. There was—somewhere in this, she felt acutely —a horror.

"That's it?" Doug said softly.

Spandecker removed his cigar stub and tossed it into the can in the corner. There was a plop and a tiny sizzling sound as the butt hit the water. Then he turned and walked into the garage. In a moment the sounds of tools clattering could be heard.

Doug, his face dark, turned to Ruth and took her arm.

They went back outside to the car, where he took the wheel again. Ruth waited until they had pulled back onto the street and he had turned west, heading out of town.

"Will you please tell me what that was all about?" she burst out finally. "And where we're going now? And what's going *on*?"

Doug glanced at her and his face relaxed only slightly. "All right," he said. "Number one, John Bartelson's widow is still alive, and she lives on this road a mile or two outside town. That's where we're going now, unless you don't want to go see her."

"Of course I want to see her. But what was all that back there at the service station?"

Keeping his eyes on the twisting road ahead, Doug told her, "I called around and found that the old woman still lives here. Then it occurred to me that there might be some things about this situation that would have been reported in a newspaper somewhere else. So I called McAlester, the daily there. I should have thought of it sooner, when I was over there this morning. I know a man in the city room."

He paused, lit a cigarette, then went on. "He pulled the old morgue file for me and read it."

"Are you talking about the file on Press Bartelson?"

"Yes. Nothing there on old John, except a death notice. But Press had quite a file."

"Was he as big a football star as people here think?"

"Yes. But what interested me was the obituary. Press died on August the eighth, 1962."

Ruth sucked in a breath. "He *didn't* go to Houston, then? He didn't—"

"He died August the eighth, 1962," Doug repeated grimly. "He died right there in McAlester, in their hospital."

With a chill premonition that it was going to be something bad, she asked, "How did he die?"

He glanced at her, then back at the road, which twisted between wooded, weedy hills. "He died as a result of a wound in a hunting accident, the story said. He had been injured—shot—several days earlier."

"*Shot?*"

"In a hunting accident."

She felt a chill. "Who shot him?"

"No way to know. There were several hunters, apparently. But that's not all."

Ruth closed her eyes. "I'm not sure I want to hear the rest."

He ignored the irony. "Press was a member of the Noble Sportsmen's Club. Great hunters and fishermen. The story made note of the fact that Press was the fourth member of the group to die within a week."

"*Four?* Within a *week?*"

"Right."

"Doug, is this a macabre joke?"

"According to the story, three members died in a car crash about the first of August of that year. Their car went over a cliff south of Noble and rolled several hundred feet and burned, trapping them inside. The three victims were Leo Huffman, a trucker who lived here with his family; Frank Tubbs, the dentist then; and Gerald Spandecker, a farmer and—"

"The man at the service station was—"

"His son."

"That's why you were asking him about his father."

"And he knows something," Doug agreed. "Or suspects something. But he won't talk about it. Nobody will talk about it."

Ruth leaned back against the seat and reached for a cigarette. She was shaken. "You think he's hiding something. You think everyone is hiding information about this—this thing eleven years ago."

"What do *you* think?" he countered, unsmiling.

She thought about it and about the evasions of yesterday and today. A chill touched her flesh.

"My God, Doug," she whispered. "What have we gotten ourselves into?"

CHAPTER
7

The storm had come, and torrents of rain smashed against the frail frame house. The windows streamed water and trembled under the wind. The outside world was an opaque fury. The roar of wind and rain beyond the thin walls made the sitting room seem quieter.

It was a three-room house—a parlor, kitchen to the rear and small bedroom off to one side. The walls were painted sheetrock, the tape showing through by its outlines, and the floors were yellow linoleum with old braided throw rugs here and there. A round-backed cane couch rested against one wall, facing a tall, cylindrical wood stove with a rusty damper pipe extended into the ceiling. There were old-fashioned straight chairs, a rocker of the type with a set handle on one side and a footstool, a love seat with handwork on the cushions, crocheted doilies on the arms. The lamps were old, too: glass bases with swirls of chocolate coloring in white and tasseled shades. The coffee table, blond pine, held a family Bible, an orange glass bowl of hard candy and back issues of *Reader's Digest* and *Woman's Day.*

Ruth sat on the love seat, leaning forward with perfect attention. Doug stood just inside the doorway to the bedroom, where an ornate dresser and gilt-framed wall mirror could be seen. In the rocker sat Gladys Bartelson, smoothing the doilies over the armrests. She had once been a big woman, but now the flesh had wasted and the blue and white print housedress seemed almost ludicrously large for her body; the skin of her bare arms, as she moved them, hung in loose folds from the bone as if she had suddenly been deflated, like a toy, almost to the point of collapse. Her gray hair, knotted behind her head, seemed too big for the rest of her. It was possible to see that once she had been not only sturdy but handsome. Now only the pale blue eyes and quick little smile remained. The smile revealed small white teeth too evenly spaced to be natural.

"You needn't be worried about the wind," she told them. "This little house has stood up to two twisters. One struck just a block or so from here. One of the big pecans in the side yard went down, but this house stood. The walls breathed, but it stood. You needn't worry."

"You've lived here a long time, then?" Ruth said.

"Oh, my, yes. Since the year after John died. That was 1936 when I moved here. September the first, in 1936. John died in December of 1935, you know. Well, Press was back from going to college that one year. He was working for Mr. Buckingham's father, the present Mr. Buckingham's father, I mean. That was a long time ago. Press didn't move out here with me. He said I was silly. But Press was like that. He loved to live in town. I didn't really expect him to move out here with me, but we owned this land. It was just about all we had left after our hard luck—that and the furniture, and then later I started getting help from welfare, after I fell and broke my hip." She sighed and patted the doilies on the chair arms. "A long time ago." Her old eyes became vacant.

"You were telling us about Press," Doug reminded her quietly.

Gladys Bartelson accepted his reminder with quiet good humor. "He was a good boy. Of course people don't remember him or my husband these days. Hard to believe they don't remember. Of course I'm old and most everyone is gone now that we used to know. But my, the way they all loved our Press! Today things are all different, rushing here, rushing there, murders, attacks on the streets, no respect. I see it all on the television. I think it's that war. Land sake, you either win a fight or you stop fighting.

It's like children on the playground. You see them move around each other and bluff, silly-like. But if they don't get to fighting after a while and someone wins, they stop. They get tired. They don't just keep circling each other for years on end. I know what John would have said. Or Press. You either win your fight or you get out. Of course I don't understand all of it, but I can't see it. What are we doing way over there anyway? Don't we have enough trouble right here at home, with people getting murdered and attacked right on the streets and showing it every day on the television?"

The storm raged outside, shaking the little house. Ruth glanced at Doug and wished for a cigarette.

Doug tried to get the conversation back on the track. "Mrs. Bartelson, someone told Mrs. Baxter here that Press owned a store of his own."

"Oh, my, yes, but that was much later. That must have been in . . . oh . . . 1954, 1955, along in there. He had a store for sporting goods. Guns, fishing poles, that kind of thing. It was a nice little store. Press loved sports. He was president of the Sportsmen's Club one year, you know. It was in those days. I think they met at his store one year. Oh, my. His name was in the paper when he opened up, his picture, about how he had played football, everything. It was just awfully nice. And for a while he did awfully well, too. I *so* hoped he would do well, not have hard luck like we did. He was always a good boy. But then, well, I don't know. Noble is so small nowadays, and I guess there just wasn't enough business, so he sold the store. Mr. Smith at the hardware, he bought a lot of the stock, and Press went to work for Latigo Oil. He had a company car and everything, drove around getting leases, checking wells. It was a fine job."

"You mentioned the Sportsmen's Club," Ruth said. "Do you remember any of the other members?"

The old woman sighed again. "Well, there was Mr. Spandecker, I remember him because I never liked him very much. Wild. A nasty man with a nasty temper. And he ran with a man named Huffman. They were alike. I hated for Press to associate with them. And then Mr. Buckingham, the one with the office now, was a member. I can't think of anyone else."

Ruth exchanged looks with Doug, then she asked, "Was Mr. Crewser a member by any chance?"

"Who, child?"

"Crewser? The druggist?"

"Well, now, he might have been at that! I know he did a lot of hunting and fishing too. He might have been, now that you mention it. I know he was a great friend of Press's."

Outside, the wind seemed to slacken, and the rain no longer pounded at the windows like a solid force. Raindrops spattered hard, continually, but the air was brighter and Ruth could see trees beyond the fence nearby, where they had left the car. Ruth tried to frame the next question she wanted to ask, but couldn't come up with the best way to ask it.

"Would you like tea?" the old woman asked abruptly.

"No, thank you," Ruth smiled, and Doug shook his head.

"I meant *hot* tea," the old woman said. "Most people nowadays, you mention tea, and they expect iced tea. I never cared for tea with ice in it. Even on the hottest days. I might not want hot tea then, but putting ice in tea always struck me sort of like putting sugar on watermelon, just ridiculous. They put ice in everything. Next they'll put ice in the bath water. We used to have hot tea every afternoon, John and I. We would have our hot tea and he would tell me about his business and it was nice. Having tea is a good thing. It settles one. Of course today people drink all those soft drinks, Coke, Pepsi, I don't even know the names of some of them. Sprite. That's one. I've seen it on the television. And Dr. Pepper. Their ads are silly."

"Mrs. Bartelson," Ruth said, knowing no subtle way to ask, "did your son have trouble with anyone in Noble?"

"Press? Heavens no!"

"When he died, was he hunting right around here? Do you remember how it happened?"

"No," the old woman replied, and her chest heaved. "It wasn't around here."

"What happened? Do you know?"

"Oh, yes, I know. They liked to hunt wolves, some. They were doing that. So it was at night. That was how it happened."

"Hunt wolves?" Ruth echoed, looking at Doug for explanation. "At night?"

Doug nodded. "They have wolf hounds, big dogs trained to run wolves. A group of hunters take their dogs out along section-line roads about dark. I went with a group once. You turn the dogs loose and they start running. You have a fire, coffee, maybe a bottle. You listen. The hounds' baying changes when they start running a wolf. You listen, and you can tell. If the dogs run too far, you start losing their sound and you get in your trucks and drive the section lines until you're close again. Sometimes the runs last most of the night before the dogs finally catch the wolf, corner or lose him."

"When the dogs catch the wolf?" Ruth asked.

"You need your guns then," Doug said, his expression distasteful. "When the wolf turns on the dogs, chances are some of them will be badly hurt or killed. Then the rest probably kill the wolf. Either part isn't pretty. Hunters have their rifles and keep track. When they hear the hounds baying, signaling the wolf has turned, the men move in as quickly as they can; they kill the wolf."

"Are wolves that much of a problem here?" Ruth asked unbelievingly.

"In years when there aren't many wolves, the hunters turn one loose for the hunt," Doug said.

It seemed incredibly stupid and cruel. Ruth suppressed the urge to say so.

Gladys Bartelson nodded. "I never liked it myself, child. Brutal, not necessary. But men are that way. They enjoy it. I know Press used to say, 'Mom, I'd like it better if the wolf didn't always die, that's the bad part of it.' He liked the chase, you see, and being with the men, the hunt. The killing he didn't want. I suppose it was necessary. Some men enjoy it."

Ruth turned away to look at the window.

The storm had continued to pass rapidly, and now the rain had almost stopped entirely, the wind was down, and a burst of sunlight flooded through the low, puffy black clouds.

She had never understood the mystique of hunting. There was a television show about "sportsmen" which her uncle enjoyed. It had always seemed grotesque to her—sunburned actors or financiers or statesmen who all looked alike in baggy clothes and floppy hats, grinning as they stalked, killed, and then chortled over creatures that flew from them in abject terror. She wondered if Doug hunted; she hoped not. To kill out of need or even out of passion seemed human. But to kill and call it recreation was an obscenity.

She was glad Press had not liked the killing, sorry he had hunted.

She asked, "How exactly was he shot?"

The old woman watched her own withered hand smooth the crocheted cloth. "No one knew how it happened, exactly. I know Mr. Smith told about it. He said several of them were together in the dark, and the wolf broke free and tried to attack the hunters, and there was shooting, and then when it was over they found Press on the ground." She looked up at Ruth, and her eyes filled silently.

It was painful. Ruth wanted to take her hand or say something *right*. She looked at Doug and saw that he was affected in the same way. He went to Gladys Bartelson's chair and awkwardly bent over her, putting his hands on her shoulders.

The old woman rallied and managed a smile. "Land sake. I'm silly."

Ruth asked quietly, "Was your son buried here?"

"Yes. Beside his father. There's no marker. I'd like to get a marker. People in town said the town ought to supply one, everyone loved him so. But then they didn't do it. I keep thinking I'll get some money saved. I will, too. He'll have a marker, one day."

Doug stood and shot Ruth a glance that had anger in it. She understood. They were caught up in this together. Noble had buried Press and tried to pretend he had never existed. It was a cruelty that filled her with a deep, irrational resentment.

"Would you like some tea now?" the old woman asked. "Land

sakes, look at that! The sun is coming out again. It was a nice rain. If you would like some nice hot tea, I can put the water on in a jiffy."

Ruth sensed they had overstayed their welcome, whether Gladys Bartelson quite knew it yet or not; they would get no more information here, and the old woman was tired.

Doug said, "We'd better be going."

Ruth stood. "Mrs. Bartelson, thank you. I know my uncle will be writing to you just as soon as I let him know your address."

"That would be real nice." The old woman smiled. She got slowly up from the chair, teetered an instant, then caught her balance and stood straight and tall. "And I hope you two will come back and see me again."

"I hope so," Ruth told her. She wondered if that was a lie— if she *would* be back.

"You won't have tea before you leave?"

Doug opened the front door, and a little cascade of rain water, trapped over it, spattered down on the front porch beyond the sill. "We'd like to do that the next time, Mrs. Bartelson, all right?"

"All right, that will be just real nice. I don't have any visitors any more, you know. I've enjoyed the visit." She patted Ruth's hand. "You do come back now, child."

They left the house and walked through the soggy grass to where the car was parked on crumbling gravel near the edge of the road. The old woman stood in the doorway of the little frame house with its high peaked roof and waved to them as they got in the car and Doug started it.

"That's a great old lady," he said softly.

"And a lonely one."

Doug pulled away, touching the horn ring. He steered the Vega along the high center of the slippery-mud section line, heading for the pavement a mile away. They were immediately driving between rows of tall old elms, cottonwoods, pecans and scrub oaks.

"It's not fair," he said with dull anger.

Ruth understood. "A lot of old people live out their last years alone."

"That doesn't mean it's fair."

"No. I didn't say it was."

"No one even knows she's alive."

Ruth did not answer him. They drove in silence for a moment. She realized that they were feeling the same distant anger and depression. Other old people ended their years in isolation and even despair, true. But Gladys Bartelson's lonely exile was different; it was tied somehow to her son's death and the others that had preceded it by a few days—and to the conspiracy of silence surrounding the entire episode.

Something very wrong had happened eleven years ago, and Gladys Bartelson—an innocent—was among those paying for it.

"The more we learn," Doug said now, "the worse it looks."

"I know," Ruth agreed.

"So do we still go on?"

The question surprised her. "I don't see how there's any question about that now."

"You have to get to Dallas."

"Dallas can wait. I want to *know* about this."

"You caught the reference to Smith?"

"At the hardware store? Yes. He still operates it?"

Doug nodded.

"Then we should see him," Ruth decided.

"I'll see him," Doug corrected her. "You'll drop me off on the way through."

She stared at him. "What do you mean by that?"

But Doug did not hear her question. Something ahead had caught his attention. "Hell," he muttered and began braking the car sharply.

She looked to the front. They had approached the intersection where the muddy section-line road intersected the narrow, marginally paved highway that led back toward Noble.

A car—a black sedan—was parked at the intersection just ahead. Someone was out of the car, flagging them down. He stood in the center of the narrow, muddy strip, waving his arm slowly back and forth over his head. He was squat, powerfully built, and wore a wide-brimmed Western-style hat.

Without a word, Doug brought the Vega to a halt in the center of the road. The figure walked toward them. Doug opened his door and stepped out of the car.

Chuck Vachon paused at the front bumper of the Vega and put his hands on his hips.

"Well, now," he said.

Doug thought he knew what was coming, in one form or another, and he felt something near gladness at the general prospect. But he knew this was the wrong place at the wrong time. And Ruth was in the car. He knew he had to avoid trouble if possible, temporarily anyway.

"Hello, Chuck," he said. "Looking for someone?"

Vachon, eyebrows knit, pointed a stubby finger toward Ruth's image behind the windshield. "I told her to forget it and be on her way."

"I could go through the ritual of saying she's done nothing wrong," Doug replied with a sense of inevitability. "But let's just save a lot of time. Are we under arrest, or is this a free-lance job?"

"Mouth off," Vachon growled, swaying like a great bear, puzzled yet dangerous. "You can lose a lot of those pretty teeth."

"You've been aching for that," Doug retorted quietly. "But I don't think this is your chance. She's a witness. A jury would listen to the *two* of us, even around here. You might get away with it, but you'd never be elected or named undersheriff again."

"You could be hurt just a *little* bit," Vachon told him.

"No, I couldn't," Doug replied quietly. "Because when you try it, I'm not going to be just standing here. I don't turn the other cheek. When you're ready, plan to come at me with everything going for you. Because nothing less than that has any chance of being good enough."

"Is that a threat?" Vachon asked, almost puzzled.

Doug laughed, a painful explosion in his throat. "What's the line they always use on TV? It's not a threat, it's a promise."

Vachon put his hands back on his hips. "I want her *out* of here."

"She's going."

Surprised, Vachon dropped his arms. It was clear now that he was not at all sure how to handle the situation, and now that his original bluff had fallen flat, he looked uncertain. In another situation, Doug thought, Vachon would have been bluntly effective. But this was daylight.

Doug told him, "I'll be sure she's on her way within an hour."

"I seen this trip out here and I thought—"

"She's leaving," Doug repeated.

"Well," Vachon muttered, "fine and dandy. My job is—" he hesitated, groping—"trying to keep it quiet. You understand? You can't have outsiders coming in here, getting people all upset."

"Right. It's a public service."

"It's a matter of—"

"Intimidation?"

"People come in here from outside," Vachon growled, "and they think they're better than we are. They stir people up, rake around in old stories that are better off left alone. It's no skin off *my* nose, buddy. I'm protecting *her,* an' people like her, that don't understand."

"If you can make yourself believe that, Chuck, good for you."

"It's the truth, you long-haired freak!"

Doug allowed his face to turn into a smile that felt tired and well used. "Can we go?"

Vachon stared at him. There was more he wanted to say, Doug saw. Vachon wanted it with him now and badly. It would come.

Vachon said, "You can go. It ain't an arrest."

Doug turned back to the car and started to get inside.

"Bennett?"

Doug looked at him.

"There'll be another day."

Doug's face heated. "I know that."

They stared at each other a long moment, and a little gust of wind made ripples in the brown-red water standing in puddles all over the slippery dirt road.

It was Vachon who turned away and strode to his car, his boots splashing pink in the standing water.

Her hands like ice, Ruth watched Doug get back inside the car and close the door. He didn't so much as glance at her. His face was colorless, as it had been in Noble when he returned to her from making the telephone calls. He was so angry that the feeling leaped from him in an invisible electric arc.

She looked through the windshield. Vachon got inside his black sedan, started it, pulled forward in a turning maneuver. The front wheels bumped up onto the crumbling edge of the narrow blacktop road. He spun the wheels and backed around, then pulled out and headed to the right, toward town.

Doug started the Vega and put the gear selector in Drive. He pulled out onto the pavement slowly, allowing Vachon's car to open a gap of several hundred yards, and then he accelerated smoothly.

"Sorry," he muttered. "Were you scared?"

"Yes," she admitted. "A little."

He smiled grimly. "So was I. A little."

She rubbed her hands together, trying to restore circulation. "You told him I was leaving."

"You are."

"No. Not now."

"*Especially* now."

"What am I supposed to *do?*" She was stung by his calm certainty that she would obey. "Just drop you off downtown somewhere and drive on to Dallas and forget any of it happened?"

"I don't expect you to do that, exactly."

"Good. Because I won't."

"You'll do as I tell you," he said.

"Men may order women around in Noble, Oklahoma, Mr. Bennett—"

"Listen to me! A Mongoloid idiot could see that this isn't a nice little genealogical research project now. Four men died back in 1962. *Four.* Half the people in this town are trying to forget it ever happened, and the other half are pretending it never happened in the first place. We don't know what it's all about. But we know it was ugly, somehow."

"That's why I'm not leaving," Ruth told him.

"That's why you *are* leaving. Do you want to be the *next* victim?"

She drew in her breath sharply. "You don't think they might—"

"I don't know. I don't know what I think about *any* of it. But I want you *out* of here."

"And what will you do?" she countered. "Stay here and try to forget, with everyone else?"

His lips went white. "Right. I'll fade into the rustic woodwork."

She regretted it at once. "I didn't mean that, Doug."

"I know you didn't," he agreed, softening.

"I just don't want to leave. It makes no sense. I know you better than you think I do. You won't quit on this now."

"Of course I won't," he agreed. "But I'm not saying you have to go to Dallas yet. You can just drive to McAlester. Or even Puntman. Just get out of this town. Let people *see you leave.* That's what's important."

"And what about you?"

Doug twisted his fist on the steering wheel as he watched the road ahead. He was driving very fast now but wasn't overtaking Vachon's car, which was not in sight. "I'd like to see Dave Smith. Also, I don't know of anybody named Tubbs in town, but there's a family named Huffman."

"One of the dead men was named Huffman."

"Right. This has to be the right family, too. She's a widow and the right age. There are three or four children. The oldest boy is a punk, and I've heard things said about the oldest girl. I'll go talk to them."

"Then what?" Ruth asked. "If she knew something vital, wouldn't she have told the police or someone years ago? Would she tell *you?* After all these years?"

"Maybe not," Doug admitted. "But I intend to find out."

"And then?" She still did not like leaving him this way.

"I know the district attorney in McAlester," Doug told her. "He's on the library board. I saw him briefly this morning, as a matter of fact. We can go to him—tell him the whole story. Maybe we can convince him to reopen the investigation."

"Maybe there *wasn't* an investigation."

"There has to have been."

"Police are the same everywhere," Ruth told him. "They like to *close* cases. They resist reopening them. We have no evidence, really, just a lot of unanswered questions."

"Spare me the lecture," Doug said.

"I was just—"

"You were patronizing me," he flared.

"No!"

"*I* know we have no evidence," he said. "*I* know we could end up looking like idiots. I don't need you telling me."

She was shocked and hurt. "Why are you attacking *me?* I'm not hiding anything. It's not *my* town."

He gave her a bitter smile. "Back to that again? I get a little tired of the sophisticated city treatment; I thought I told you that."

"And I," she flared back, "get just as tired of people in this part of the country still fighting the Civil War and thinking New Yorkers aren't white."

"Fine! Then get the hell out!"

"I will!"

He slammed the car around a curve. She stabbed at the ashtray with her cigarette, partially missed, and showered hot sparks on her own legs. He ignored her as she patted out the sparks with angry slaps.

Ahead were the first houses of town. Doug eased off the speed slightly as they flashed past several old shanties and an abandoned warehouse building. The road became a street, widening and getting rougher, old bricks. The silence was thick enough to cut, and Ruth chased her own thoughts in a tumult of bitterness and surprise. All at once everything was completely wrong. She was furious with him.

Trying to get her thoughts collected, she was caught off guard again when the Vega swerved and slowed abruptly. Doug swung it quickly to the curb, tires shrilling. He hurled the gear selector into the Park position and turned to her, one arm over the back of the seat.

"All right," he said disgustedly. "I'm a stupid idiot."

She didn't understand. She stared at him.

"I blew up for no reason," he said, as if goaded. "I'm not mad at *you*. I'm mad at people being close-mouthed and lying when possibly the whole thing isn't even that serious. Like I said, I'm just an idiot."

She was so relieved and he looked so irritated with himself and so flushed with resentment that her nervous laugh barked out before she knew what she was saying.

"I guess I've known bigger idiots," she told him.

He grinned. "Damn you anyway."

"I'll tell you what," she said, and it was all right again. "I won't say your town is hicky if you won't say I'm a callous, pushy Yankee—or something equally bad and sinister."

His grin broadened, got into his eyes. "Deal."

She took a deep breath. "Deal."

The car engine was still running. He ignored it, leaning back and resting his hand on the top of the steering wheel. "My feeling is that there might be some danger here. Don't ask me what or how. Four people died. There's been a lot of covering up. Things like this can happen. Somebody could have been murdered. *All* of them could have been murdered. A lot of people around here are scared half to death that you or I will find out something about it. That's why Vachon tried to scare you and that's why someone messed up my car. Now, if we're completely wrong on all this, and there's a logical explanation, we can both putter around here for days before we find it, or we might *never* find it. But if there *is* something—and *someone*—then how do we know you aren't in genuine danger?" He stopped and frowned. "I think you ought to get out. I'd feel safer about it. I can check with Smith and the Huffman family and meet you in McAlester, say, by late this afternoon. Then we either get some interest from the law, or we take another look at our hole card."

"You really think someone in this town is capable of what you're talking about?"

He glanced at her quickly, betraying new surprise. "Of murder?"

"Murder—or whatever it might be."

"Yes. People are capable of anything, anywhere."

"I don't know if I can *believe* that."

"Not intellectually," he pointed out. "But what kind of *feeling* are you getting from this?"

She hesitated, and a coldness was in her body.

"You can't tell what anyone may be like, or what he might be capable of, from seeing him on the street," Doug pressed. "*Yes,* someone here could be capable of killing. I think almost anyone is capable of it if he's pushed far enough, desperately enough. Which is why you have to leave."

Ruth thought about it. She knew he was making sense. "All right."

"You agree?" He looked surprised.

"I agree with you every once in a while," she told him mildly.

He smiled and started the car down the street again. "You can drop me and go on. For appearance's sake. You can take the ridge road, the scenic one. It's faster to the Interstate. Check in at the hotel. I'll be there this afternoon. We'll go to the courthouse."

"What if we do that—and they don't believe us?"

"I don't know," he snapped, almost angry again.

"Are we making it all up?' she asked. "*Is* it all just small-town distrust of strangers and something we don't fully understand? Are they all just jealous of their memories?"

Doug looked at her a moment. Then he returned his gaze to the street. They passed the Spandecker service station with its clutter and approached the railroad tracks beyond.

Finally he said, "I don't think it's our imagination. Every little town has its secrets. I know Noble better than that. I don't believe this is . . . " He paused and seemed to hang up on his thought processes. The Vega bounced over the railroad tracks.

"All we can do," he said more firmly, "is just what I've said. You go to McAlester. People will see you leave."

"You couldn't just go with me now? The Huffmans probably aren't important."

"It's important for people to see us separate."

"I don't like it," she told him passionately.

"I understand that."

She saw that it was the only way. A blackness spread in her

body—a sensation so deep and primitive that she had no way of coping with it. She shuddered.

He pulled onto Main Street and drove past the real-estate office, the post office, the drugstore. He parked beside his rented winch truck, put the car in Park and got out. The window was part way down and he leaned inside as she moved to the driver's side and adjusted the seat forward.

"Go out south here," he told her smiling in a casual way she knew was for anyone watching. "The second turnoff to the left has a scenic marker. Just follow the ridge road. You'll come to the Interstate direction signs in about fifteen miles. It's only a couple of miles farther where you get on the highway. And I'll see you there this afternoon."

She looked out at him and felt suddenly very much like crying.

He reached inside. "For appearance's sake," he said. He took her hand and shook it.

His hand was warm and very strong. She didn't want to let go. "Be careful," she pleaded.

He stood back from the car. "Maybe the only danger is our imagination anyway. Drive carefully, and we'll be embarrassed later after we find out how simple the explanation really is."

She put the car in Reverse and backed out. Doug stood on the sidewalk, holding the smile she knew was bogus. He waved. She returned the gesture and pulled away, turning around the great old stone building. There were more railroad tracks. The Vega shimmied over them and she felt a burst of utter hatred for the town, for its rough tracks, for its shabby buildings, its lying, its deep-layered atmosphere of isolation and suspicion and hidden memories.

She had come here, she thought suddenly, only yesterday. She had never felt this way in her life. She had lost all sense of reasonable normalcy. It was as if she had completely lost her moorings.

She had seldom had any trouble believing, in New York, that there were people nearby who were quite capable of the worst kinds of violence; there was obviously all that evidence, and it was easy enough to invest a faceless stranger with vicious desperation. But here in rural Oklahoma it seemed so unlikely that one would find a sinister situation, especially one involving long-held secrets with blood on them. And how could she invest any of these people here with the ability to murder? Was it possible to imagine Alvin Crewser as a cold killer? Or Paul Buckingham? Or even Vachon?

They seemed not *big* enough, she thought, not larger than life, not driven by pressures of sufficient magnitude—not even given the sort of opportunity that the density of the city provided. Was it really *possible* that whatever secret they seemed to share, or suspect, was even very serious?

Driving faster as she quickly reached the edge of town, she lighted a new cigarette, rolled the window up and touched the air-conditioner button. New billowy dark clouds were rolling in. Another squall line, or whatever they called them in this godforsaken end of the country, was moving in. She inhaled the smoke of the cigarette deeply and settled back in the seat.

The town was behind her now, and she had passed the first county road turnoff. She glanced at the odometer and saw she had about seven-tenths to go before reaching the scenic route Doug had suggested. Already, out of Noble, on her own again in the car, she felt better.

A lot of it, she told herself, had been self-hypnosis. She had experienced an odd sort of disassociation at other times on trips in strange motels, in strange cities or towns. Away from the usual people, the usual surroundings—all the comforting minor routines, the regular gasoline station, regular doorman, regular buildings along the way, recognizable radio and television personalities—it was possible very quickly to feel some of one's own superficial personality ebbing away. It was as if one became a different person, a person almost without identity in some superficial aspects, just because all the surroundings were so different, seemed so remote from what had come to be considered "reality."

She wondered how much of what had happened in the last twenty-four hours was like that.

Ahead was the scenic route turnoff, a small blue-on-white sign pointing left. She slowed and turned, moving onto narrow, newer asphalt with high-graveled shoulders. The road immediately began to wind and rise, and ahead she saw the hills, an unexpectedly lovely panorama blue on the distant horizon, with great slabs of cloud in the misty distance.

She held the speedometer on 55.

It was entirely possible, she thought, calmer now, that her questions had simply irritated people. She knew she had a way of seeming brisk. She had come in a stranger, poking around, and they had resented it, so they had lied.

They had very little to remember, she thought. Press Bartelson had been a hero who died foolishly in a hunting accident. His father had committed suicide. The same week Press had stupidly died, three other local businessmen—perhaps drunk—had run their car off a road and killed themselves, too. It made a silly, unpretty picture. It made all of them look just a little hapless. And Press, especially, had been the one person of all who had given Noble a few hours of pride.

Thinking about it in this light, she saw how flimsy any other possibility really was.

Behind her on the twisting road, an ancient Dodge pickup truck with flapping fenders, repainted a dirty chocolate brown, began to gain rapidly. She watched it in her mirror for an instant, then returned to her thoughts and the road ahead.

It was going to be embarrassing, talking to a judge in McAlester, she realized. In this new frame of mind she had adopted, she wondered how Doug Bennett had ever accepted her suspicions even for a moment. It had been unpleasant for him, too. But there were plenty of explanations for someone crippling his car. He had been wrong when he said someone here might be a killer in hiding. It was simply impossible.

The brown truck was directly behind her now and extremely close. With a feeling of irritation, she released pressure on the gas pedal to let him pass. She had just topped a rise, and the high-banked rock fill on either side dropped sharply between hills, while ahead the road turned slightly to the left, going down steeply toward a bridge, little more than a railed slab over a weedy ditch, at the bottom.

The brown truck moved out beside her.

Doug, she thought, should have been smarter than she had been. He should have pointed out all the inconsistencies—

With a sudden swerve, the brown truck moved toward her.

Nerves jangling, she jerked the wheel to the right, but there was no room—the right front tire hit loose gravel and tried to bite in, carrying her wider—into the sickening drop.

The truck's battered front fender crashed into the side of the Vega. Two wheels hit the gravel, and Ruth fought desperately for control. She was aware of a man staring at her incredibly close—through the broken window of the truck on her side.

The truck bounced from the impact, veered out in the road, slowed, and then suddenly came toward her again, at an even more deadly angle.

She knew without thinking that she had only two choices. Something—a combination of instincts and experiences—told her instantly that the truck would hit her broadside, sending her over the chill drop, if she slowed or braked.

She floored the accelerator.

The Vega engine screamed as the transmission dropped into lower gear. The wheels spun for a fraction of a second and then the rear end swung out to the left, crashing heavily into the truck. It veered and rocked toward the far side of the road again, and Ruth had the Vega past it, rocketing down the hill with the speedometer winding toward 80.

She didn't know what was going on, but she was badly scared. The truck—

The back window of the Vega exploded. Wind shrieked in, throwing papers all over the interior. There was glass everywhere, and she saw a crack in the windshield. The road hurtled by in a blur and she glanced in the side mirror and saw a figure leaning out of the truck window on the passenger side, with a long tube.

They had *shot* at her.

Stunned, she had no time to think. The Vega plummeted down the hill toward the twisting little bridge. She had the accelerator on the floor. The truck was following hard, perhaps even closing the gap. Going into the turn, she clung to the wheel, pressing hard on the brakes, hearing the tires scream complaint, and then she remembered to take the turn onto the bridge as tightly as possible. It was no sports car, but she had driven an old Morgan for a year, and she knew how to make a car drift. She went into the curve. The wheels seemed to float on the smooth pavement and she felt it going, but she maintained some control and then the car bottomed out, hitting the maximum extension of its springs as it went over the bridge and the road ahead twisted sharply, left again and then right, going on down with trees on both sides, little graveled shoulders and ditches.

The truck hove into view behind. It had gained. Ruth pressed the accelerator without thought, her own car widening the gap again slightly, whooshing over a little rise and then plunging downhill again. Trees flashed past in a continuous blur, and she was fighting the wheel because the road twisted tortuously, going lower through the deep series of wooded ravines between hills.

She had to get away—somehow widen the space between herself and the old truck. But she knew, with sinking terror, that the pursuing vehicle had a new, powerful engine under its decrepit hood and must even have special springs that allowed it to corner faster than her low-slung sedan. She was not pulling away from it despite the fact that she was driving harder than she had ever imagined anyone could and stay on the road.

Then, flashing around a curve and almost losing control, she knew that it *didn't matter* to her pursuers whether they caught her or not. Their intent was to drive her off the road. Whether they did it by pushing her off or pressing her beyond the limits of her skill or the car's cornering ability made no difference. The roadway was remote, deserted. Doug had said it was more than ten miles. Whether she allowed them to catch her—or pressed harder and crashed—it was the same to them.

Who were they? *Why?* There was no time to try to understand.

An S-curve sign flashed past on the right. She slammed hard on the brakes. The Vega careened sickeningly, two tires crashing off into the gravel on the wrong side, and then she slid out of control an instant, the rear wheels hurtling back across the roadway sideways, and she had it under control again, but the brown truck was right behind her, and then her windshield shattered and air and fragments of glass gushed in against her and she couldn't see for a moment, and she jammed her foot full on the brake in panic, and it was all a nightmare now; she had been completely wrong to imagine the feelings of Noble had been illusion—*they were trying to kill her.*

The Vega swerved, its wheels locked. The roadway spun and vaulted sideways, trees blurring by, and she knew the brown truck was beside her, crashing into her again. She was skidding. She was off into the gravel—a lurching moment of being airborne as the Vega cleared the small ditch—and she saw rocks out one side; she was out of control, off the road, smashing into heavy brush—little trees going down and the rending of sheet metal, a series of bone-jarring bumps as she was battered by the shoulder harness, and she thought in the chaos, *They've done it— I'm being killed.*

And then suddenly the car was at a stop, its front wheels out in space over a creek bank. There was a hissing of steam or escaping air; she was sitting in a blanket of shattered glass that glittered like jewels from the sun slanting through the ragged edges where the windshield had been, and she felt absolutely nothing.

She heard, distantly, the sound of movement in the high brush that was all around the car. She knew only that she had to get away. She turned on the seat, scattering shards of glass, and tried to get the door open. It was wrenched and stuck.

Two figures pressed through the high brush and walked swiftly toward her. They both carried guns—rifles or shotguns, she didn't, in her shock, know.

One of them walked to the door, peered in at her, and then jerked the door open.

The other, gesturing with his gun, said with husky sadness, "All right, missy. Get out of there now."

It was only then that recognition seeped through her battered consciousness. The one who had opened the door was the man from the service station, Ted Spandecker. And the other, pale but resolute behind a bolt-action rifle, was Paul Buckingham.

CHAPTER 8

Once he had seen Ruth's car out of sight, Doug Bennett turned and walked halfway up the block to the hardware store owned by Dave Smith. He went inside the packed, old-fashioned building and had to go all the way to the back—past long rows of garden tools and a Black & Decker display—before he found anyone in sight. A gawky youth stood behind the counter that displayed Smith's lethal offering of rifles and handguns.

"Is Dave here?" Doug asked.

"Nope," the boy said. "He's out this af'ernoon."

"What time will he be back?"

"Dunno. He went huntin'. Can I he'p you?"

Doug declined the offer and left the store. It was a setback, but a minor one. He had not expected any real help from Smith anyway.

He went back toward the city building where he had parked the rented pickup with the winch assembly on the bed. It crossed his mind that the winch truck was a note of absurdity that could happen only in Noble. The truck somehow seemed to stand for the unreality of the whole situation; he wondered if he and Ruth had made a big melodramatic thing out of nothing.

He didn't think so. There were too many coincidences, all bad.

Rejecting the idea of calling the Huffman house because of the chance of being overheard, he opened the door of the truck to climb inside. As he did so, two men came down the steps of the city building. One of them was a round man with a cookie-duster mustache. His name was Roscoe Ansley and he was the city clerk.

"That your personal bookmobile, Doug?" he called.

"Temporarily, Roscoe."

The other man, John Drummond, a mortician who was in his third term as mayor, walked loose-jointedly around toward the back of the truck and peered at the winch. "Mighty upliftin'."

"Oh no!" Ansley winced.

Drummond winked. "As mayor, I could use all that pull."

"Maybe," Doug suggested. "You could call it City Haul."

Drummond looked blank for an instant.

"Haul!" Ansley yukked. "Haul! H-a-u-l! Get it?"

Drummond sighed and walked away. Ansley gleefully followed.

Grinning, Doug watched them saunter up the street into the next block, where a bread truck from McAlester was unloading at the grocery. How well we hide the things really on our mind, he thought.

Starting the truck, he backed around in the street and headed north off the square. Like everything else in Noble, the Huffman house was not far away. Doug knew it—one of five frame ranch houses that had been built one next to the other at the same time back in about 1960, when local merchants were proclaiming Noble on the way back to prosperity. The houses had been built on a long slab of red clay slowly eroding into an abandoned oil-well site in the weed field to the west, so that the houses stood high from the narrow gravel road and well above the trashy oil site, away from everything else by fifty yards or more. They hadn't been good houses to begin with, and the people who had bought them had neither the money nor the taste to maintain them. As Doug approached them now, he saw that one had a concrete block addition built on the side, so that it looked a little like a service station; another was painted a bright orange with yellow shutters; another had never been painted at all; and a fourth had a rickety picket fence around the entire yard—front and back—as if to keep the tricycles, wagons, trash drums, boxcar racers, swing sets, clotheslines, sandboxes and wind-twisted mimosa trees from sliding down into the gulch.

The fifth house in the line, at the far end from the road, was the one he sought. It needed paint. There was no lawn and no real driveway, simply a muddy furrow across a side of the weeds. The front screen door stood rusted out against the wall near the tiny slab porch. There was a small Honda motorcycle parked at the side. Aluminum foil gleamed in some of the windows, including the front picture window, which had been placed to provide the worst view and maximum exposure to the afternoon sun.

A few spatters of fresh rain hit the truck windshield as Doug drove into the yard and parked at the corner of the house. He felt a little better to know Ruth was safely on her way to McAlester, but it also felt lonely without her. Maybe here he would learn something to lay the mystery at rest. He got out of the truck and walked to the front door. He pressed the door chime button and, hearing nothing except the distant racket of a television set, rapped sharply on the door.

After a moment the door opened. The dark air that spilled out was wet, with the characteristic fetid odor of a water cooler in use in an area where humidity was too high to make it effective. The boy who looked out at Doug was short, painfully slender, wearing only a pair of Levis hanging on his bony hips. Pale hair hung down in his eyes, which looked sleepy and hostile.

"Yeah?" the boy said. He was about sixteen and practicing being cool and tough.

"Is Mrs. Huffman here?" Doug asked.

The boy put one splayed bare foot on top of the other. "Who wants to know?"

Behind him in the room a girl's voice asked, "Who is it, Leo? Is it Jack?" A girl somewhat taller than Leo, with long dark hair and pretty eyes and a wide, coarse mouth, bounded up beside him and looked out at Doug. She wore a pair of shorts and a halter and was plumply well put together.

"You're not Jack," she said, grinning. Then she struck what

she probably thought of as a seductive stance. "What can we do for you?" she asked, giving him a quick up-and-down look.

"I'm looking for Mrs. Huffman."

The girl cracked her chewing gum. "Selling something?"

"No," Doug said.

"Bill collector?"

"No."

She pursed her pouty lips. "You're *not* one of those guys that goes around praying over people, are you?"

"No." Doug smiled.

The boy, Leo, said gruffly, "I'll check if she's home."

"Oh, shit, Leo," the girl said. She pushed the door open wider. "Come on in, honey. The old lady's back in the utility room. Go get her, Leo."

"Go get her yourself," Leo said as Doug stepped into the living room. "I'm tired."

"*You* go get her, you little bastard," the girl shot back, "or I'll tell her you've got a stash."

Leo glared at her and doubled up his fists.

"Go ahead and hit me," the girl said, smiling. "Then I can make *sure* you're put away where you belong."

Leo grunted something under his breath and stormed out of the room, heading for the kitchen beyond.

Doug stood inside the front door. The living room was perhaps ten feet square, with a threadbare blue rug and yellow walls. Jammed into the tiny space were a green velvetlike couch, a black leather recliner chair, a smaller red-flowered rocker, two end tables with huge porcelain lamps and ashtrays on them, a magazine rack stuffed with old copies of *Life* and *House Beautiful* and confession magazines, a coffee table with an elephant TV lamp, a battered Philco television console and a large red-and-white imitation leather hassock sitting slightly askew, as if a little deflated on one side. Several baby pictures hung crookedly on one wall, while on another there was a four-foot cardboard replica of a painting of a mountain scene that never had been and never would be.

Looking around at this, Doug came back to the girl. She stood beside the couch, watching him. Her eyes tested him.

"I'm Sally," she told him. Everyone here, it seemed, acted. She was playing Ann-Margret.

"I'm Doug Bennett."

"You live around here?"

"I work at the library."

"Gaw," she breathed, smiling at him. Then she dropped to the couch and extended one suntanned bare leg along the cushions so that her plump thighs were spread, stretching the material of her shorts to the maximum. "You're the *librarian?*"

"Yes," he said.

She made a little wet sound with her lips and teased two fingers gently along the inner line of her thigh as if without thinking. The movement managed to be totally obscene. "I'll have to come down there and check something out from you."

From the kitchen came a middle-aged woman in an outfit not unlike Sally's. Her graying hair was tied up with a small length of ribbon and she looked careworn, with deep circles under her eyes. Sweat filmed her face, and as she walked in Doug saw that her thick legs were purple-lined with varicose veins.

"You want to see me?" she asked, unaccountably nervous.

The boy came back into the room and leaned against the kitchen doorway, picking his teeth.

Doug introduced himself again. "I'm filling out old news files at the library," he told her. "There's very little information on your husband's death, and I hoped you could provide some details."

She sat wearily on the edge of the couch, pushing Sally's leg off, and mopped at her face with the towel she had carried in. "What kind of details?" she asked suspiciously.

"Anything you can tell me, actually. About all we have is a story saying your husband and two other men died in a car accident."

She looked at him, and her mouth set. "That's all there is to tell. He's dead. The first week in August 1962. August the second. He wasn't driving, if you're an insurance agent or looking for a way to file another lawsuit or anything like that. We've been through all that. We got nothing from the insurance, but that was on the physical exam technicality." Her voice was flat and bitter. "If he had been driving, it wouldn't have happened. Leo could drive. He drove a truck for a living. So if that's what you're looking for, forget it."

"I'm not looking for anything like that," Doug told her, "and I'm not a lawyer."

"He's our librarian," Sally purred, giving him a feline smile. "Isn't that nice?"

"You behave yourself," Mrs. Huffman said.

"I know how to behave, Mom," Sally said.

"Yeah," Leo grunted in the doorway. "Like a punchboard."

"Leo, leave the room! She's your sister! I won't have you talking like that!"

"Why?" the boy countered sullenly. "Because you know it's true?"

"Leave this *instant!*"

"It's boring here anyway." Leo yawned and slouched to the front door. "I'm gonna go riding."

"Not without your shoes and helmet!"

He looked at her with the kind of open contempt that exists only in the family. "Bull," he muttered and went on outside, slamming the door.

Mrs. Huffman turned toward the door, her face working. The sound of the Honda blatted in the side drive. "That boy!"

"He's a hateful little prick," Sally said. "That's what he is."

"Sally, I don't want to *ever* hear language like that from you!"

"Why?" Sally grinned, shooting Doug a glance to see if he was impressed. "After all, Mom, I'm a big girl. I *do* know what—"

"Go to your room! *Go* to your *room, instantly!*"

Sally sighed and uncoiled her legs. She gave Doug another smile and walked out, round hips swaying. Ann-Margret again.

"I apologize," Mrs. Huffman said to Doug with a pathetic smile. "It's the storm. They're both very high-keyed, and they've both been sick; they're going to summer school, getting a good education. But there's a virus."

Doug nodded sympathetically although he knew it was a lie. He felt a surge of pity for this weak, tired woman trying to raise a son intent on becoming a thug and a daughter already, perhaps, a whore. "You were telling me about the accident," he prompted gently.

She sighed. "There's nothing more to tell."

"Exactly where did it happen, Mrs. Huffman? And what time, if you know? And how?"

She sighed again and looked off into space, her hands clenched in her lap. "The worst time, of course. When it happened, I mean. We were all so excited. Of course Leo never liked him; he hated him, I think, and it used to scare me, the way he talked. But I always said he wasn't so bad. I even voted for him, but I never told Leo that. He would have . . . " Her voice trailed off on whatever she had started to say.

"It was on the old mine road, where it happened," she resumed with an evident attempt to get hold of herself. "You know where it turns along the river and runs along the side, high up? That was the place. The three of them were in the car. The Spandecker car. It was a new Dodge. I remember, he was so proud of it, electric windows and everything. It was late, after midnight. They came along there and missed the little turn and just . . . went off."

"What had they been doing out there?" Doug asked, puzzled by several of the things she had said.

"I don't know," she admitted, eyes blank. "They hunted sometimes at night. Sometimes they had a wolf hunt. I know the very same night, south of town, Press Bartelson was hurt in a hunting accident. He and some others were hunting wolves and he was shot by mistake. He died a few days later. Maybe Leo and his friends were on the way to go on that hunt, too. Or maybe they had had their own. The dogs weren't along, but if they were with other people—"

"Press Bartelson was hurt the same night your husband was killed?" Doug asked, wanting to make sure of this. "It wasn't a night or so later, possibly?"

She shook her head. "No. It was the same night. We all remarked about it, it was so unnecessary. With all the excitement, the whole county fixing up and getting ready, and the newspaper and TV people already coming in, it was going to be the biggest day in our history. Why, Frank Tubbs was even on the Noble welcoming committee. What was he doing out hunting the very night before? It was all so senseless! Leo, of course, said he wasn't even going to attend. But I thought he would, at the last minute. And then they were all killed, and in all the excitement the next day, it hardly rated more than an item in the papers anywhere."

"I don't understand," Doug said, watching her intently. "In all what excitement? What was going on here the next day?"

She looked at him and her eyes widened. "You don't remember?"

"I was away at school that year."

"Why, that next day was the day the President came to dedicate the road!"

"The President?" Doug echoed, thunderstruck.

She mistook his tone for ignorance. "The President of the country! John F. Kennedy! Don't you remember when the President came to Noble to dedicate the scenic highway?"

When he left the Huffman house and drove off the little red clay plateau overlooking the oil rig, Doug did not turn south, as he had originally planned, in a direct line for the road that led out of town. He headed instead back downtown. He was having a hard time keeping his thoughts and feelings in any kind of order.

Before he headed for McAlester to join Ruth there was now one more step to be taken. The weekly newspaper had published a special memorial edition on the day of John F. Kennedy's visit to Noble. Published late on the afternoon of the unlikely event, it had been specially produced with the help of several part-time photographers and writers hired on a one-shot basis from other small towns in several counties. Doug remembered the copy in the library files; jammed with special (and profitable) congratulatory advertising, it had been a sixteen-page paper, large by the usual Noble standards, and filled with pictures and stories about the day's events.

There would, he thought, be a story on the auto crash and Press Bartelson's shooting in the edition somewhere.

But he was not interested merely in that, because by now he had had a brainstorm.

The violence of that night in early August eleven years ago made no sense as an isolated incident. Would it make more sense if related to the President's visit?

On the surface it seemed a comically unlikely circumstance. But nothing else had made sense. Perhaps this last big incongruity would somehow provide a trace of a pattern. *Three had died. One had died. The President had visited.* How could they relate?

He would get the memorial edition from the files and take it to McAlester with him.

It was raining again, hard, as he drove down Main Street. Despite his tension he felt a pang of hunger and remembered he hadn't eaten. It was now well into the bleak afternoon. He would stop at the drive-in on the way out.

Pulling up in front of the city building, he remained in the truck a moment, hoping the pounding sheets of rain would slacken before he had to run for it. He noticed there were no other cars along the curb here and wondered where Vachon had gotten off to. He hoped he didn't find out.

Waiting, he mulled briefly his new information. It remained tantalizing, disconcerting.

Huffman, Tubbs and Spandecker had died in an unlikely automobile accident late at night, presumably on the way back from—or to—an unlikely hunting outing of some kind. About the same time, in an unlikely parallel accident, Press Bartelson had been shot.

And the next day—most unlikely of all—the President of the United States had come to Noble.

Was he, Doug wondered, going off the deep end when he thought there had to be some kind of connection? Was the timing of the events only another in a seemingly endless sequence of coincidences?

The rain continued to drum upon the truck and stream down the windshield. He decided to run for the side door.

He opened the truck door and was instantly drenched. The rain spanged into his flesh, chilling him. Turning, he started toward the sidewalk that led between the building and the abandoned grain elevator next door. As he took the first step, he saw the side plank door of the grain elevator building swing open.

Dave Smith, his face shining whitely through the driving rain, waved for him, gesturing some sort of appeal. Smith was hatless and drenched, but he wore an olive-drab slicker-jacket.

His voice came through the pounding of the rain, and Doug got only one word, a tattered fragment: *"Help!"*

As the word came, Smith staggered backward in the doorway and appeared to fall.

Veering off the sidewalk, Doug ran to the side door, which flapped open in the gray opacity of the driving rain. He thought he saw Smith on the dirt floor inside and, with a muttered exclamation, rushed through the doorway.

The storage-barn section of the elevator complex was tall and black and musty, smelling of rain. High bare planks glistened on all sides from rainwater tearing through bright grayish rents in the lofted roof far above. The light was sufficient to see the object on the dirt floor, and as Doug took his second step inside, he saw that the object was not Smith—was not a man at all, but an old burlap bag.

Mistake, he thought. *Bad mistake.*

And he spun toward the doorway he had entered, but it was too late.

There was a quick flash of blurred movement and he saw the figure coming but had no time to react. Something heavy and hard and unbelievably painful smashed into the side of his skull. He knew he was falling, felt the pain spread out from his head and face through all his body, and the pain turned crimson and then yellow and then black, and he fell into nothingness.

CHAPTER 9

The impulse was to scream—to scream and keep on screaming, to let the fear burst out. Ruth fought it and held it back by the tiniest margin of control.

The tunnel was less than ten feet in diameter. The only illumination was an urnlike, battery-operated fishing lantern on the loose gravel-and-earth floor. Its yellowish light shone against chalky stone walls, seeping water here and there, braced in X patterns with heavy, rough-cut timbers gone black from age and rot. The planked roof sagged, as if ready to surrender to the crushing weight of the hill overhead. At irregular intervals a great 10 x 10 length of oak, ax-marked, had been wedged vertically under the roof planking to help hold it in place. The tunnel curved into blackness beyond the penetration of the lantern, and except for the occasional sifting of dust through the planks overhead, as the earth seemed mysteriously to shift slightly, it had been silent a very long time.

Ruth, her hands tied in front of her, was made prisoner to one of the huge support beams by another length of rope looped through her arms and tied to the beam. Her legs were free. By stretching the ropes to the maximum, she was just able to lean weakly against the tunnel wall.

On the other side of the tunnel, less than six feet away, Doug Bennett lay face down in the gravel, his head in a small, syrupy puddle of blood. His hands were tied like Ruth's, and he was held to a post in the same way she was, although it seemed unnecessary; he had not stirred in all the time since they had brought him in and dropped him there.

Sitting on old crates on the fringe of lantern light, Ted Spandecker and Dave Smith held a silent vigil. Neither man had moved or spoken for a long time. Spandecker was pale, and his eyes stared into vacancy with a gaunt preoccupation. Smith, a stubby man with a tight burr haircut, looked more at ease in his light hunting clothes and soft yellowish boots; but his face was grimly set, as if he were at some kind of war with himself to maintain complete separation from any of this.

As Ruth watched him, his eyes suddenly swiveled and met hers. He seemed to be coming back briefly from a private place, and his recognition jarred her into speaking.

"How much longer is this going *on?*" she asked huskily.

"Shut up," Smith said.

"How much *longer?* What are you going to do?"

Smith's eyes were like slate. "I'll gag you if I have to."

"At least let me help Doug," she pleaded. "My God, what harm can *that* do?"

Spandecker told her, "You'd better do like Dave says. He means it. He'll stuff a rag in your mouth if you keep after it."

Ruth stared at them. She had seen the quality of their expressions before, but only in photographs. The pictures had been from war; they showed men in a lull in battle, their bodies seemingly relaxed, yet with an inner tension that betrayed itself in the staring isolation of their faces as they looked privately into things the viewer could not imagine or comprehend. Spandecker and Smith had that quality about them now, and it was a thing not quite human. They were in their way as afraid as she was—and that was most terrifying of all.

It had been hours—Ruth had no way of knowing exactly how many because her watch had been broken—since Ted Spandecker and Paul Buckingham had taken her from the wrecked Vega, put her in the truck and brought her here. It was an abandoned mine, its mouth boarded off and covered with legal warning signs, its approach choked by weeds and fallen boulders from the sharp-rising granite hill above. Spandecker and Buckingham had pried a few boards loose from the entrance and dragged her inside, tying her here. Then, refusing to reply to any of her questions, Buckingham had guarded her while Spandecker kept watch somewhere outside.

Much later there had been a series of scrambling sounds outside, about forty yards past the curve in the tunnel that blocked all view from this spot. Spandecker, with his rifle, had come back to summon Buckingham, and both men went outside, taking the lantern and leaving Ruth in pitch-blackness. She sat there, straining to hear the words of what seemed to be a hasty colloquy with some third person.

In a little while Buckingham had come back with the light, placing it on the tunnel floor where it sat now amid the rubble of years fallen from the ceiling. Then, as Ruth had struggled to readjust her eyes to the light, there had been a sound of heavy footsteps and grunting in the tunnel beyond the curve, and Spandecker—with a man she now knew was Dave Smith—struggled back with the limp form of another man supported between them.

As they dropped him on the floor and began tying his hands, she recognized Doug.

That had been the very worst moment, because she was sure, seeing the bloody wound on the side of his head, that he was dying. That had also been the time she screamed, and Smith had instantly slapped her hard across the face, his eyes going crazy with panic.

Smith's panic had stilled her. She saw, numbed, that the panic made him and the others capable of anything.

"How bad is he?" Spandecker had asked, looking down at Doug.

"I don't think as bad as he looks," Smith had replied.

After that she had managed to maintain a semblance of control.

In a few minutes after Smith's arrival with Doug's unconscious body, Paul Buckingham had had another whispered conversation with Smith and Spandecker and then left. He had not been back.

Smith and Spandecker had remained here, evidently as guards, and with the exception of an occasional silent visit to the front of the tunnel, as if to watch for someone, neither man had done more than sit against the wall, gun in hand or nearby, watching.

For hours.

Doug, breathing slowly, was still unconscious. With her other fears was a mounting horror that she would have to watch him like this until his breathing stopped. She knew Spandecker and Smith were waiting, but for what—or for whom?

The same questions had been echoing through her mind forever.

She sat up and watched the two men guarding her. Smith stared into space, his face set and grim. Ted Spandecker's much more youthful face was clammy with sweat, and he kept looking nervously from Doug's form to Ruth.

The next time his nervous eyes came to hers, she spoke. "Won't you just let me see if I can help him in some way?"

Smith's eyes swiveled again. "Last warning."

"I could bandage his head," Ruth said. "I could try to stop the bleeding."

Smith looked at her with eyes like steel balls and did not reply.

Spandecker rubbed a big hand on his knee, betraying his nerves again. "Why not let her?" he asked huskily.

"No," Smith said.

"It wouldn't hurt anything."

"No," Smith repeated.

"I don't see why."

"You don't have to see why. This is your first time."

Spandecker's face went slack. "You talk like there are going to be *other* times."

"How do we know?" Smith retorted bitterly.

"Listen, Dave, one time is bad enough, but—"

"We don't *think* there will be anything more," Smith replied harshly. "But we didn't think so the last time, either. You just can't know. Once it's been done, it just goes on and on, or it stops. You should be smart enough to see that. There's no turning back."

Spandecker glanced at Ruth, then licked his lips as if they were sandpaper. "I couldn't go through any of this twice."

Smith grunted a laugh that was macabre in its lack of any feeling but revulsion. "I said that too. You learn. One thing you learn is, talking doesn't help. There's no way it can be nice. But if it comes, you do it."

"We were wrong. We should have waited—made sure."

"How long would you wait? Until one of us was in the electric chair?"

Spandecker took a deep breath and straightened his back. "What time is it?"

Smith held out his arm and let Spandecker read the watch on his thick wrist.

"It's time, isn't it?" Spandecker asked.

"They'll get here when they get here. Now shut up, I said!"

Spandecker shot another brief look at Ruth, at Doug, and then hung his head, staring at the pebbled earth between his boots.

Ruth controlled herself with a total effort. She had *known*—she had been aware of what they must plan—from the moment she was taken from the car and brought here. Each event had amplified the belief. Now there was no doubt.

She and Doug had been brought here for only one purpose. They were to be killed.

She tried to convince herself that there was some other possible outcome. But there was none. She and Doug had meddled into something old and ugly. They had had their warnings, in the lies and vagueness first, and then in the more obvious threats such as the tampering with Doug's car. Now, whatever this was about, and whoever was involved, a decision had been made: She and Doug had gone too far, learned too much, gotten too close to the central truth of it. These men were holding the two of them here now while decisions were being made or arrangements concluded.

There would be some new accident.

She tried to imagine it. They would have been content if she had died in the wreck when the Vega left the road. Their first idea must have been for her to leave the road where it was high and the plunge surely fatal. Then they would have dealt with Doug in some other way. But that hadn't worked, and now both of them had been brought here. Perhaps that explained the delay. The conspirators—however many there were—faced the problem of making the accident appear convincing.

How difficult would that be? In her case, not difficult at all. It could be an auto accident after all; her body could be taken back to the wrecked Vega. Perhaps they would take both her and Doug back there. She imagined the little news story: "*A young amateur genealogist from New York and the Oklahoma librarian who was assisting her were killed today when her car left the road. . . .*" Or something else—they could simply vanish; she would not be missed, perhaps, for weeks. The people in Dallas would be irritated more than worried—would hire someone else to do the spec layouts. Doug? Did he have any family who might quickly miss him? She doubted it.

The prospect was so astonishingly simple and clear that she reeled before it. These things *happened*. They were not illusion or fantasy. And now it was happening to her, and she was going to die, and Doug might already be dying.

If only he were conscious, she thought despairingly, she could cling to a meager hope. Hadn't he told her he had been a Ranger or something in Vietnam? She remembered things she had read about Special Forces combat teams, their training. Doug had seen combat. If he were awake and able to function, he might do something. He was capable. She had sensed this frequently and known it without doubt when he faced Vachon at the road near Gladys Bartelson's house.

But he was not conscious, could not help.

Another hour or more passed. Without daylight to guide her, she had no idea whether it was day or night but knew it must be dark outside by now. Death happened in the night.

Finally she almost dozed. Her entire body throbbed with pain from bruises in the accident. Her clothing was soaked and chill and she felt feverish. Her consciousness ebbed, came back, slipped from her again. The nightmare was going to last forever.

Then, with a closeness that startled her badly, came the sound of a low-pitched whistle. She sat up, wide awake again, shaking.

Spandecker got up and reached for his rifle. Smith's head jerked up and he listened hard, cocking his bull-like head.

The whistle repeated itself.

"They're here," Spandecker said huskily.

"All right." Smith's jaw set as he picked up the lantern, making gargoyle shadows dance on the wet walls and roof of the tunnel. "Let's go meet them."

Spandecker nodded and went first toward the curve in the tunnel that shielded the view from here to the outside. Smith followed, the battery lantern bobbing at his side. The light faded and then went out, like a snuffed candle.

In the pitch-blackness, Ruth heard her own teeth chattering. She was going to scream now. She knew it. She was losing all control.

Then the voice whispered sharply nearby: "Ruth!"

"What?" she gasped. "Who?"

"Keep your voice down,'" the other voice hissed, and now she recognized it. "Listen to me."

"Doug?" Gladness tightened her throat. "My God, I—"

"Be quiet and listen!" he whispered fiercely. "We might have only a few seconds!"

Her heart in tumult, she obeyed. All she could think was that he was *alive*, he was conscious, and there was a hope. She was not alone.

"I've been awake a long time," his whisper told her, and in his voice there was a steely calmness that she marveled at. "We might have a better chance if they think I'm half dead. Tell me where we are."

"It's a mine shaft," she whispered. "I don't know exactly where —it's into a big hill, and they said something about Hempstead—"

"Hempstead One," Doug whispered. "All right. They went to the entrance just now?"

"Yes, it's not far."

"Okay, I know exactly where we are, then."

"Doug, how did they get you?"

"I was stupid," he said bitterly. "No time to tell you now. Just listen. There's going to be *a time*. I don't know when or how. It will come. You'll have a chance of *some* kind. When you get it, you have to break that lantern. Kick it. I may not give you a signal. You'll just have to know."

"How can I know?" she whispered, horror creeping back again like spring ice. "How can I—"

Sounds came from the mouth of the tunnel—timbers being moved, muttering voices and boots in gravel.

"You'll know," Doug told her. "Kick hell out of the lantern. Run for the front. These support timbers are ancient. If I lunge everything against it, I think it will go down. The roof may come in, I don't know what. But I'll get loose. In the dark I'll try to follow you."

"But what if it *doesn't* fall?" she hissed. "What if—"

"*Hssst!*" he warned her.

The footsteps were closer, and the first faint traces of illumination stained the curve of the tunnel walls.

Trembling, Ruth watched the light grow. As it neared the curve, it made her position bright enough to allow her to look at Doug. She was amazed—almost thought she had been hallucinating. He lay absolutely as before, his face still in the pool of cold blood, eyes closed.

The sight now, however, did not frighten her. It sent a bolt of hope through her veins. They didn't know he was all right, she thought, and they didn't know the kind of man they were dealing with. There *was* a chance.

The lantern, carried by Smith as before, appeared in the curve of the tunnel, half-blinding her. She saw in the glare that there were at least two more men. Smith walked close to her, put the lantern on the pebbled earthen floor about where it had been previously and moved to the side to let the others form a rough semicircle across the width of the tunnel.

With Smith was Ted Spandecker, of course, looking more pale from his brief exertion. The new men were Paul Buckingham—and Alvin Crewser.

It was a shock, and then immediately Ruth wondered why.

She had been prepared for Vachon. But Crewser should not have been unexpected. Perhaps part of the surprise was his dress: black from head to foot, heavy cotton trousers and a body-fitting nylon shirt with a turtle neck. His boots were heavy and competent, and he carried a military-style carbine with a leather strap. He looked for all the world like an aging movie commando. The thought gave her a wild impulse to laugh.

Paul Buckingham, wearing a dark sweat shirt and baggy brown trousers, nodded with quiet recognition. "Here they are, like I said."

Crewser glanced at Doug. "Is he dead?"

"No," Smith answered.

Crewser's lean face showed no emotional response one way or the other. His eyes turned to Ruth. They were haunted. "You had to keep poking," he said. He sounded very tired.

"Why have you done this to us?" Ruth asked.

Crewser expelled a heavy breath. "You left us no choice."

"All I did was try to find out about a dead man's son!"

With a slow, weary gesture, Crewser shook his head. If he had looked any less like the appealing man in the drugstore, she might not have recognized him. There was a terrible weight upon him.

He said, "Until you went to see Press's mother, we still hoped you would just go away. Then we knew it was too late." His eyes were bright with pain and resentment. "All you had to do was leave it alone. We didn't want any of this to happen. But you wouldn't stop."

"Now you're doing this to us," Ruth shot back, "and I still don't even know what it is you're hiding!"

Crewser's eyes were dead. "You know enough. You were going to raise questions—stir it all up again. We could see that."

Watching him, Ruth saw that she had underestimated him and perhaps all of them. They had been watching, trying to wait. Crewser did not want this to be happening. Yet he showed the same bitter stoicism she had detected in Smith. *It's too late now*, that look said. She saw that she was trapped and that Crewser and his companions felt just as trapped and helpless as she.

They were all caught together in it now, and none could turn back.

Somehow this realization of their feelings made the fear multiply, because she saw that *nothing* could stop it now.

"What are you going to do?" she asked thickly.

Crewser looked at his three companions. "What are we going to do," he repeated. "A very good question."

Smith said almost angrily, "We all know what we have to do."

Crewser nodded. "But the method is the problem. It would have been much simpler, Paul, if you had done things right on the road."

Buckingham's head jerked. "She's a good driver. You didn't tell us that. She almost got away."

"I didn't know that."

"We did our best. We almost killed ourselves, and then when she was alive, we did the best thing we knew to do, bringing her here."

Smith asked flatly, "Does it matter?"

"No," Crewser said, watching Ruth. "Of course not. Not now."

Spandecker asked hoarsely, "Isn't there *anything* else we can do?"

It was as if he had not spoken.

Crewser stood still, deep in thought a moment. "Every minute we're in here," he said finally, "our risk is greater. We've had plenty of time to think about this. Does anyone have a new idea?"

Paul Buckingham licked his lips and said hesitantly, "I think we could just leave them here."

Crewser eyed him without response in his expression. "Leave them here?"

"Take them—take them deeper into the shaft," Buckingham said quickly, the lantern light making his eyes glow like coals. "It's boarded up—people don't come in. It might be years before anyone finds them—maybe never."

Smith grunted, "Kids play in here. Clear up to high-school boys. They're not supposed to, but they do."

"But if we took them far back—"

Crewser shook his head. "It won't work. They would be found

sooner or later. And how would we explain *that?* The two of them, tied?"

"We could—" Buckingham stammered "—we could—he's already knocked out, we could knock her out—"

"No," Crewser said. "I see why you want it this way, Paul. It takes the act away from us. We simply leave them. No more violence. I understand that. But it won't work. We have to be sure."

Smith said, "There's a deep shaft back there someplace. If they went down t re—"

"They might still be found," Crewser said. "And how will anyone account for the two of them having been in here? No. It has to be an accident. Better, two accidents."

The three men stared at Crewser in silence, and Ruth felt her heart lurching in her throat. To hear them calmly discussing how her *death* was to come—

Smith asked, "What will we do, then?"

Crewser hesitated and then gave an almost imperceptible nod, accepting command. "Paul," he said, "you'll take Mrs. Baxter back to her car. It's out of sight and hasn't been spotted yet. She'll be found in the car tomorrow sometime."

Paul Buckingham smoothed a quaking hand through his unruly hair. His jaw hung open. "I can't do it," he rasped.

"You've got no choice," Crewser said. "No more than any of us, now. Spandecker will go with you. It can be a head injury, or her throat can be cut by broken glass—"

"I *can't!*" Buckingham cried and began to sob. Hideous, rasping hysteria burst out of his chest. He shook. Tears filled his eyes.

Smith said grimly, "I think it would be better if I went with him. Ted is nervous too."

Crewser looked at Smith. "Are you sure?"

Smith's thick neck seemed to swell for an instant, and then he nodded.

"All right," Crewser said. He gave Buckingham a flinty look. "Did you hear that?"

"Yes," Buckingham sobbed. "But I don't want any part—"

"I've already told you!" Crewser flashed. "*You have no choice!*"
Buckingham stared at him, and his sobs suspended.

"It has to be done," Crewser said more softly.

Ted Spandecker said, "What about him?" and nodded toward Doug, still apparently unconscious on the ground.

Crewser scowled. "He'll have to be a hit-run victim. It's thin, but it's the only thing I can think of. We can drive him almost to Puntman and leave him on the highway."

"How will we explain—"

"We won't," Crewser snapped. "It will be a mystery. But what reason would anyone have for suspecting? He's a war veteran, a drifter. When asked, we can tell how he was moody, unpredictable." For a split second he donned his usual demeanor, and to Ruth it was shockingly as if he were standing again in his drugstore as he mimicked speaking to a reporter or policeman. " 'Doug Bennett? Yes, I knew him. Moody sort. Very strange. Always did strange things, walked alone at night, came and went for no apparent reason.' " Crewser dropped the pose and became grim-visaged again. "It will have to do."

Smith nodded. "It *will* do."

"All right," Crewser said, taking a deep breath. "Dave, you and Paul take the girl first. We'll wait one hour and then leave with him. After you do what has to be done, go directly home. Stay there. Make it a point to call someone in town for something or other. That might help later."

Buckingham nodded and wiped his face on a handkerchief. He was trying pitifully to cope. "All right. I can do that. I have some properties—"

"Good. Anything else?"

Smith, Buckingham and Spandecker stood silent, their faces ghastly in the light of the lantern at their feet.

"All right," Crewser said. "Tomorrow there will be no telephone calls, no conferences. If we meet, we meet. If we don't, that's fine too. It will all be just fine unless someone cracks."

Smith shook his head. "No one will crack," he said, shooting first Buckingham, then Spandecker a sharp glance.

"All right," Crewser concluded.

None of them moved. They looked like ordinary little men, and that very quality made it so much more terrible.

"Now?" Smith finally breathed, as if he were very tired.

Crewser nodded.

Smith took a blunt-pointed hunting knife from a scabbard on his hip and took a step toward where Ruth was tied.

"Not *here!*" Buckingham choked.

"I'm just going to cut her loose," Smith snapped nervously.

Ruth was unable to remain quiet. She was thinking of what Doug had said—*there would be a time*—and it was very near. She was terrified she would miss it, do the thing badly, end it instantly. She had to postpone it somehow, and the only way she knew was to blurt out the question that had tortured her for hours.

"*Why?*" she asked.

Smith paused, standing over her. His face wrinkled in perplexity.

Crewser spoke. "I told you. You learned too much."

"*You* killed Press Bartelson and those other men?"

Crewser looked genuinely startled. "We didn't kill Press. *They* did."

"They?" she echoed numbly.

"The three of them. We think it was Huffman whose gun actually went off first, but there was no way to tell because naturally we had to start shooting then."

"Press was on *your* side?" Ruth said, trying to see the insane pattern.

"Of course," Crewser said, as if surprised again. "Hadn't you figured *that* part out yet either?"

"You people here?" she stammered, trying to see all of it and still baffled. "You killed Huffman? Tubbs?" She remembered the other name and looked, stunned, at Ted Spandecker. "*Your own father?*"

"He was a child then," Crewser said, as if embarrassed by her accusation. "Naturally he had no part in it."

Ruth stared, incredulous, at Ted Spandecker. "These men killed your father—and now you help *them?*"

Spandecker's face flamed. "Nobody will *ever* know what kind of a man he was—what he would have done! I can do this—protect his memory—"

"They killed him, and now you help them *to protect his memory?*" Ruth's voice rose shrilly because it was hopeless; there *was* no pattern; she couldn't understand any of it.

Crewser snapped to Smith, "Get her out of here."

Smith nodded and bent over her. His knife snicked the rope. "Get up," he said.

Ruth struggled to her feet. Her legs were weak and she felt dizzy. Smith took her arm and pulled her toward the others—toward the tunnel curve and entrance beyond.

"You go first," Smith grunted to Buckingham, who stood frozen.

Buckingham, sweat dripping from his chin and nose, nodded. He gave Ruth one ghastly glance and moved toward the blackness beyond the lantern pool.

Crewser and Spandecker stepped back against the wall to make way as Smith pushed Ruth ahead of him.

And the time was now.

She was beside the fat, red-plated battery lantern on the ground.

My God, she thought, *if I do it wrong—*

"Come on," Smith said, nudging her again from behind.

"I wish it hadn't happened," Crewser told her. "I mean that."

Ruth scarcely heard him, because she was in motion.

She kicked the lantern with all the force within her. It was heavy, and the shock of impact staggered her backward, off-balance, catching Smith by surprise so that he staggered. Crewser barked an expletive and Spandecker started to move. The lantern careened across the floor and crashed into the wall and went out.

Ruth had already spotted the direction she must move, and she lurched forward in the sudden pitch-blackness, bumping into someone. Hands grasped at her. She screamed and clawed at the unseen face, feeling her fingernails gouge flesh and eyes. The man yelled hoarsely and she was free, staggering ahead in the blackness, bumping into a timber, going around it. Where was

Buckingham? Crewser was shouting sharp orders, and Smith, too, was yelling, and then there was a *grating* sound behind her, and someone yelled more sharply, and a huge, crumbling impact exploded everywhere as parts of the roof came down, tons of aged dust gushed around her legs as she stumbled on toward the opening and escape. He had done it. Doug had pulled the beam free, and in the black behind her it sounded as if the entire hillside were falling down into the tunnel. She saw a faint oval of starlight ahead and ran, falling and getting up and running again as the earth quaked.

CHAPTER 10

When the tunnel went dark and Doug threw his entire weight against the roof support post, he knew his chances were virtually nil.

For a number of reasons: the post might not budge; one of his captors might grab him immediately; the post might go, but fall in such a way that he couldn't slip the broad-noosed rope off either end, or the post might go, but the ceiling with it.

Almost all the bad things happened, but in a good combination.

When Ruth kicked the light against the wall, Doug was ready. He rolled over and got his legs under him as the light vanished. Using the back of his shoulder to absorb the impact, he threw himself against the post with all the force in his body. Just as he moved, someone grabbed for him, but his motion caused the attacker to miss catching a firm hold and stagger into the post just as Doug hit it intentionally.

The post went with shocking quickness. It fell so easily that Doug was carried down on top of it against the wall.

For an instant he thought the mountain was coming down. Tons of earth and loose rocks dropped into the tunnel, burying his legs. Someone screamed. Doug recognized Spandecker's voice and knew he was hurt. Crewser was yelling orders, but someone else was yelling at the same time, adding to the chaos.

Frantically, Doug felt along the post for the nearest end and managed to free the rope that held his wrists to it. He kicked his legs out from under the huge, loose cone nearly filling the tunnel as more dust and gravel and soggy earth sifted down from above. He felt, in the dark, that the tunnel was half closed toward the exit by the great mound of debris that had already fallen. He scrambled over the mound on his belly and rolled down the far side, his feet striking someone's legs. Dave Smith shouted hoarsely and clutched at him. Doug swung around as he rolled to his side and lifted his elbow sharply. It cracked into Smith's jaw in the dark and he was momentarily loose.

On his feet now and a little dizzy, he groped through the heavy dust. Someone collided with him and ignored him. Spandecker, behind the pile of dirt somewhere, was screaming in pain. Doug moved forward, found the curve in the tunnel and followed the wall with his bound hands. He wondered why he couldn't see the opening ahead and then he realized his eyes were shut—had been shut the whole time. Opening them, he saw the faint oval of night at the entrance.

Reaching the opening, he climbed over the partially dismantled plank barrier and slid on his hip down the brief shale incline that led from the entrance. It was fully dark, with a few stars overhead and some low-scudding clouds. He could make out only the larger surface details. He rolled into a rock and sat up, slightly dazed, twenty feet below the tunnel mouth. He was still on the hillside, which slanted through brush toward a creek valley a hundred feet below and loomed overhead fully three hundred feet to a lumpy, tree-studded summit. Other hills and earthen cliffs stuck up black in the night on all sides. He knew he had only moments to make a decision and strike out in one direction or another, but he had to find Ruth.

From the mouth of the mine above, someone—Smith or Buckingham—shouted. Doug moved into the brush to his right, and as he did so he saw a quick movement just ahead.

"Ruth!" he snapped.

"Doug?" came the reply. "God, I thought—"

He caught her hands, also still tied. They were icy and she was sobbing, her face a pale, blurred oval. "Are you hurt?"

"No. I—"

"This way!"

He headed down the embankment at a crazy pace, taking little care about the possibility of falling. The bushes and weeds were about waist high, with only an occasional scrub evergreen taller. There was no chance of escaping by stealth. He had to get to the creek at the bottom—deeper cover—before anything else could be considered. If they got that far—

Behind and above, a rifle pammed, then another. Running half blind, Doug had no idea where the bullets were going. He cut to his left, smashing through heavier cover, and then saw an eroded ditch just in time to slow, jump it and drag Ruth over behind him. She fell heavily, one leg dropping into the ditch so that she sprawled on the lip, and only his help prevented her going all the way into the thing. Going to his knees he dragged her bodily out of there and into some stickery bushes.

"Okay?" he asked.

"They're *shooting* at us," she said as if she couldn't believe it.

"I noticed." He pulled her to her feet and ran again. Two rifles banged close together, and this time he heard one of the slugs, well off and high. He cut to the left and then to the right, avoiding any sort of straight path they might anticipate. The rifles hammered again, and then came three or four lighter sounds, spiteful, some kind of pistol. The bullets tore up leaves and brush all around them, hitting dirt and rocks and singing off. Doug had no time to look back; he could hardly see the next step in front of him. It was amazing that they could see down into the gully at all; in addition they were peppering them with a series of near misses. Ordinary men wouldn't have seen, couldn't have fired. Crewser, Smith, Buckingham and Spandecker might be ordinary in many respects, but they were night hunters, Doug reminded himself—and desperate now.

Only a few yards ahead, the hillside flattened and then plunged into the totally black brush clinging to the narrow creek. Doug feinted to his left, as if heading for some rocks, and a volley smashed the bare earth ahead of him. He swung back sharply to the right, sprinted for the ditch, grabbed at Ruth with his awkwardly tied hands and hurled her forward into the heavy cover.

Propelled by Doug's body force, Ruth simply plunged into the blackness ahead without any control whatsoever. Leaves and branches struck her face and then there was no earth under her feet and she fell forward, going head down, tumbling down the wet, leafy bank, striking a small tree with her hip, turning around and falling head over heels once more before she hit, with a splash, in a rivulet of warm, gritty water. She rolled over, coughing and spitting. She and Doug were all tangled together. He helped her sit up and she got the coughing stopped.

The water murmured around them, only inches deep. No other sound came from anywhere. Her heart crashed around in her chest as she struggled for air. From the faint starlight filtering through trees overhanging their position, she could see that the creek ditch was quite narrow, with precipitous walls covered by vines and leaves. She had no idea which side they had fallen down or where the danger now lay.

Doug, his head strained at an angle, was listening. Trying to calm her breathing, she fought for stillness, instinctively hoping to assist him.

He leaned so close his lips touched her ear. "There's a pocket knife in my left pants pocket. Can you get it?"

He turned on his hip to allow her awkwardly to work her hands into his pocket. She pulled out some keys and change and the little knife.

"Open it."

With pain-stiffened fingers she managed to pry open the single small blade, and then, as Doug held up his wrists, she sawed furiously at the rope binding him. The small blade sawed through. He took the knife from her and freed her hands. Pain tingled into her fingers with the relief of full circulation.

"Okay?" he whispered.

"Yes." She amazed herself: Her reply sounded calm.

Doug crawled out of the water and onto the bank, climbing on his belly. She followed as best she could, seeming to make much more noise than he.

He crawled up the bank to the top, gave her a cautioning gesture and peered over through the brush. She scrambled up and lay beside him, wet and shaking.

The view was back up the steep hillside they had just come down. She recognized the profile of the hilltop against the starry sky. Trying to pick out the mine entrance, she caught a brief movement in the darkness. Her breath froze in her throat.

Doug saw it too. She felt him tense.

There was another movement, and then she saw a third.

Three figures were coming down the hillside—one in the center, near the dark splotch she imagined was the mine entrance, another about twenty yards to the left, the third an equal distance to the right. They came slowly, moving with evident caution, and she could not hear a sound. They were halfway down the hill and moving toward the creek ditch.

As one of the figures moved briefly against an open patch of sky, she saw the man-silhouette clearly, and the rifle barrel held across the chest, pointing upward. She chilled. How often had she seen that stance and kind of movement in films showing hunters stalking prey? The three of them—perhaps the fourth somewhere out of sight—were coming down calmly, formed in a line, *coming for them.*

She wondered where the fourth man might be. Had he been hurt, or was he circling around, or had they perhaps sent him to the cars to make sure no attempt was made to take one of them for escape? There was little chance to reach the cars, she realized; their flight had taken them at an angle well away from the one necessary to get to the clearing where the dirt road had led from the highway. And now the line of three men—perhaps more—effectively blocked off any attempt to go in that direction.

Looking at Doug, she saw his intense concentration. She knew he was trying to guess where the fourth man might be and what their plan was. He had to respond. She was glad it was his decision, not hers. The countryside on all sides appeared equally bleak, broken, formidable. She knew she would have had no chance alone. He might know the area, and once more she remembered those few words about his military training. She clung to that.

Making some decision, Doug leaned close to her. He whispered, "Be just as quiet as you can."

Then, without awaiting a reply, he turned and started back down the ditch wall, on his back, digging his heels into the soft earth to go slowly.

She followed, doing her best. Twigs split beneath her, leaves slid, pebbles tumbled and splashed. Hc was going silently, she thought bitterly, and she sounded like an elephant. It seemed impossible the hunters could not hear her agonized progress.

Reaching the bottom again, Doug promptly began climbing the other wall, the far side. He got up to the top with seeming ease and reached back, pulling her up the last few feet with surprising strength. He gave her no time to rest, immediately getting to his feet in a crouched position, looking right and left, and then moving off in a straight line ahead. Small trees stood here and there, the brush was taller, and the incline was lashed in all directions by erosion marks, some several feet deep. Her eyes fully accommodated to the night now, Ruth could see everything with great clarity. She stayed low, following Doug's zigzag course as he hunkered along, climbing. Behind them there was no sound.

By the time they were halfway up the hill, a distance of more than two hundred yards, she had begun to believe they would get away. The brush was taller and heavier, with more trees, and they were in a ditch higher than their heads. The ditch slowly played out and they came out in an upsloping field of slender scrub-oak trees that would surely screen them from the eyes of pursuers. Ahead were a pair of vertical earth or rock cliffs, at a distance, that stood like spread bookends, and the jagged hint of other cliffs against the sky.

Leading her by the hand, Doug moved higher.

Behind them, well down, a male voice sounded. It carried with shocking clarity in the deep night still. It sounded almost conversational. *"There they go."*

Another voice called in the same calm tone, *"I see them."*

"All right. Fine."

Doug seemed not to hear. He kept climbing steadily. Ruth's flesh crawled as she awaited the impact of a bullet in her back.

But there was nothing.

So they were in a new phase, she realized slowly. The time for foolhardy shooting at a distance, in bad visibility, had ended. The men behind her had formed a better plan now.

They were stalking.

They were that sure of themselves, she thought. She fought the incredulous terror trying to reduce her to hysteria.

She continued to climb behind Doug, her tired body working like a robot. Part of her was still trying to believe that none of this was happening.

These men behind them, who meant death—who seemed so very *good* at this—were, incredibly, the same ones she had met in Noble. She could not relate them in those roles to this menace. Alvin Crewser had seemed kind, moderately intelligent, ordinary. Paul Buckingham, his eyes on a past that would never be again, had been so ineffectual. Smith and Spandecker had seemed unremarkable, too. Neither they nor their dying little town would rate a single slide on a vacationing family's Instamatic. Yet now, here, the same four men represented death.

Trying to come to terms with it, she realized she still did not understand precisely what had happened here those eleven long years ago—the events that were as alive and present tonight as if the eleven years had never been. The four "ordinary" men now behind her somewhere in the darkness had killed. Tonight Ted Spandecker would not lean on his gas pump and talk earnestly about Fram oil filters; Crewser would not dispense cough medicine or hand out cigarettes from behind his antique cash register. Tonight their other side was here, and they would kill if they could.

On one level, suddenly, it all made perfectly good sense. Ruth followed Doug, scrambling up a steep shale hillside, hidden from any possible observation by trees below, and she saw that he was taking her into rougher terrain, where vision would be blocked continually by rock formations, tall trees, cliffs and hillsides and ravines. She was hurt, the terror was ice in her belly, her hands were torn by thorns and raw earth, her knees burned from scrapes, her breath sobbed from her lips. *She* was not the cool, urbane intruder she had been a day ago either, she saw. She was like them—like everyone. The layers had been stripped away and now there was no pretense, and beneath the veneer they were alike. They could kill, she thought suddenly, but *she* might kill, too, if she must—if given a chance. There was in each of them, buried deep, the same ancient beast, Hesse's Steppenwolf, waiting. People who said there was no wolf, she saw now, were the worst of fools: They had never looked steadily into the hidden lair of their own heart.

Doug drove her mercilessly. Time passed and she managed to keep up. In a little while—a quarter of an hour?—they had reached a chasm between nearly vertical cliffs where centuries of rain and wind had stripped the earth to jagged outcroppings, like shattered platters protruding horizontally from the cliffs on either side. The passage where they momentarily rested was very narrow, so dark at the bottom she could not see Doug's face as she caught her breath.

"This won't do it," Doug whispered. "I can't shake them."

"Maybe we already have," she said. "I can't hear them or see them."

"They're back there."

"But we can't be sure."

"*I'm* sure."

She accepted it; he *knew*. He understood everything that was happening far better than she. He understood the terrain and how they were moving and the men behind them. She would have blundered straight along, but already he had turned several times for no apparent reason, perhaps outguessing the maneuvering of the silent killers who followed.

Now he spoke as if to verify this, his voice taut and very low.

"They've split up. One of them has gone ahead. He'll be up there where you can see the tall trees."

She looked ahead through the gash in the vertical rocks and saw overhanging bluffs on either side perhaps a quarter of a mile away. "Waiting for us?" she guessed with a shudder.

"On top," Doug affirmed.

"How do you know?"

"He made a slip. I saw him off over there."

"What do we do?"

"There's only one way. I can't move fast enough this way. We have to split up."

She stared at his shadow. Her insides quaked. *"No."*

His head moved as he looked sharply upward at the walls on either side. "I've got to climb this thing. Do you think you can?"

"No! But—"

"Listen to me, then! There's no way they can see you in this dark, if you stay in tight against the rocks and brush and don't move."

"You want me to stay *here?*"

"It's our only decent chance."

"I can't! Doug, don't ask me to do that! I *can't* stay here; they'll *find* me."

"I'll climb out," he told her grimly. "Now *listen*, Ruth! I'll climb out. I'll move ahead. I know where one of them will be waiting. I can take him. The others will hear it and hurry. Maybe I can get them, too."

She stared at his shadow, her heart a heavy sickness in her chest. *"Maybe* you can?"

He ignored her question. "You'll hear the commotion. By that time, if the others have gone by this spot, you start back the way we came. Remember the gully just back there? Go into it. There's a little waterfall and a cave. Hide. I'll come back if I can."

"If you *can?*" she echoed, fighting hysteria. "What if you *can't?*"

"I shouldn't have said that. I can. We'll be all right."

He was grimly lying to help her, and she saw it. "I want to stay together."

He hissed in warning and squeezed her hand so suddenly she winced. His head was up, cocked to listen.

Her blood whispering in her temples, she knelt in the rocky earth and listened too. She heard the faint rustle of wind in trees and somewhere the distant call of a night bird. Insects chirped incessantly all around them.

"They're coming," Doug told her. "Look. Move back in here, see?" He separated some heavy dead brush against the rock wall.

She obeyed, but as she did she was trembling horribly. "I don't want to," she told him. "I want us to stay together."

"Remember," he said, pressing her down against the cool, dry rock walls that formed a box covered by leaves and branches. "Wait. You'll know when to go back. Wait in the cave."

She tried to cling to his hands. She was begging him.

Gently, firmly, he pulled away. He was only a shadow looking down on her. It was like the last stage of a nightmare, when everything had gotten worse and worse for what seemed like forever, and now it was time to awaken. But it was real; there was no awakening. The funny little men had become dealers of death and she had nowhere to run to and now she was to be alone.

Doug stood, pulling his hands away from hers. She made one last desperate attempt to reach out for him, but he moved away and became a shadow, and she shrank back in her little hiding place. She knew now they were lost. She fell back against the jagged rocks. *Let it be over, then,* she thought with a burst of bitter anger. *God, just let it come and be finished. No one should have to face this any longer.*

Taking a slow, deep breath, Doug looked up at the rock wall. He caught, distantly, the tiny sounds the men were making as they came up the ravine behind him. About two hundred yards, he thought: about where the other gully intersected, and they might pause a moment there, making the obvious choice. He could picture them moving carefully, fighting the anxiety and forcing themselves to hunt calmly, as if their game were a deer.

Dave Smith was the one who had gone ahead, Doug thought. By now, Smith was probably almost a half-mile away, moving at breakneck speed along the ridge line to get to the trees up ahead.

There were only two men coming through the gully. This meant someone had been hurt or killed in the tunnel cave-in. Ted Spandecker had been the one who screamed—the one who was deepest in the tunnel. So Spandecker was out of it.

That left Crewser, Smith, Buckingham. Crewser was in charge. He would send Smith ahead; Buckingham could not be trusted to do things correctly. Crewser had Buckingham with him; they were the two coming along now from behind.

Knowing this, however, was little real help. It left Doug's problems essentially the same.

Finding what appeared to be the best route up in the darkness, he went to the cliff face, reached up and tested one of the platterlike projections jutting from the earth and rock of the face. The edge of the shale crumbled as he tested it, making a shockingly loud miniature landslide. It was no better than he had expected.

Doug bent down, pulled off his shoes, placed them back in the weeds out of sight and reached up to a heavier-looking projection on the rock face above his head. Keeping fingertips well in toward the thickest part of the rock, he heaved his weight, caught grips with his toes, which could grip through his socks, and began climbing.

He hadn't climbed since Nam. Some people did it for a hobby. He considered them insane. Now he wished he had taken it on for a hobby himself. It might have made this easier.

Resisting the temptation to work too closely to the cliff face, he held on with one hand and groped higher for another solid handhold. Finding one, he moved a few feet higher. Tiny pebbles and bits of debris sifted down every time he made the slightest movement. He found a slanted crack in the rock and worked upward a number of good holds, climbing swiftly.

In the daylight, he thought, the cliff would be an easy practice site for amateurs. There were handholds everywhere. Breaking apart in layers as it was, the cliff offered no difficult smooth areas.

In the dark, with the need for haste, it was different. Much of the rock was too rotten to bear weight. He could not pick the best route up. He had to go on feel, and he didn't know how long it would be before Crewser and Buckingham came into the ravine behind him and could look up and see his dark silhouette against the cliff.

If they spotted him here, he had absolutely no chance.

He kept moving, maintaining balance and not staying in any one place more than a few seconds. He was doing fine, he told himself. Giving himself a pep talk. It wasn't such a bad little cliff; he had scaled much worse.

He was a third of the way up now, however, and already fatigue was taking its toll. Sweat made his shirt cling cold to his back and shoulders. His hands and toes had begun to sting from abrasions, and the first dangerous tremors were starting in the large muscles of his thighs. The front thigh muscles warned you first. They were sending the first warnings now.

Clawing upward with fingers like spider legs, he caught a thick projection, balanced himself, tested with a little weight. The platter broke clean. His arm swung free and outward and for a split-second he was going. The panic of falling gusted emptily in his belly. He clutched at the earth for another hold. The broken rock bounced heavily off his shoulder, pebbles and dirt showering his face and head, and then it tumbled loudly to the ravine floor below. It splattered and broke, and little rivulets of dust sifted down. He caught another hold and swung into the rocks, gladly letting them gouge into his chest and hips.

Taking a breath, he set his teeth and reached up again, found the raw, sandy spot where the last hold had broken loose and located another just beside it. Forcing himself, he tested this hold in the same way. It held. He lunged upward, trusting it, and his upswinging left hand found something to grasp, he got his right foot planted, and he was that much higher again.

The rock face sloped away from him slightly and he could almost crawl the next twenty feet or so. He hurried. They had to be nearing the turn behind him now.

Leaving Ruth below was the worst. He didn't know if she could handle it. If she stayed very still—made no sound—she had an excellent chance. He had not deceived her on that count. With luck he would be well ahead by the time they passed her hiding place; he might even be upon Smith by then. Unless she panicked and gave herself away, they would go right past her. Then it was up to him to make sure they did not get to retrace their steps.

She had stayed up with him far better than he had hoped she might. Asking her to handle this, however, was hoping for a miracle. If he had had a rope, or even the remotest thought that she might be able to climb with his help, he would not have taken this chance. But it was this or nothing, and, imagining her fear alone below, he felt the primitive anger build in his gut.

Another handhold broke loose, but before he had put much weight on it. Shale slid loudly down the face to silence and the dark below.

He was well beyond the halfway mark. Some of his fingers were bleeding, making holds slippery. His upper thighs were afire with painful fatigue. He was beginning to understand the rock now and almost felt a bitter liking for it. He and the cliff were all that mattered, and they were in an intimacy. It had been waiting for him all these centuries, sun-warm and then bleeding earth moisture that froze and broke in tiny shards, waiting for him to come. He clawed higher, his warmth soaking into the rock, his sweat being absorbed by its pores. It had to do nothing; it was like a woman, and he attacked it with soft and loving strength, feeling for its innermost secrets. It allowed his touch in silence and waited. It would see.

The sky seemed nearer. He was within twenty feet of the crest. An earthen lip overhung the top, tufted with thick prairie grass and weeds. Slender trees stood near the edge, some of their branches overhanging the abyss. A spider or tiny lizard, startled by his hands, scampered over the sheer rock only inches from his face. He very nearly started backward in shock. A few pebbles tumbled down from under his toes. They rolled and bounced free and fell in silence, then hit and rolled again, and finally were still.

His hands felt raw. He gripped and seemed to have strength, but feeling was going from them. He swung higher again, got his feet planted, raised his own seemingly massive dead weight by sheer will power on the dead stumps of his thighs. A little ledge was just at the level of his eyes and he got his elbows over it and hauled himself up. An easy one. He stood on the four-inch shelf, hanging onto a knobby rock with his left hand and a tuft of dense brush with his right, his forehead against the warm cliff.

It was not far now. Ten feet. A few more moves and he could reach it. He was doing fine, he lectured himself.

Far below, there was some vague little sound.

Staying close to the rock, he turned over his shoulder and tried to see. Looking back was always a mistake and he knew it. But it was necessary.

He could not see the bottom. The rock face sloped straight down and out of sight into blackness. He could see the far cliff wall vaguely, and in one direction he could look along the rim toward the winding, brushy ravine they had followed. The other way, he could see the overhanging lip of the wall and the starry sky beyond. He felt suspended. His pores shrank from the empty space that seemed to suck at his back.

For an instant a sense of incredulity swept over him. Two days ago his most serious concern had been finishing some indexing. If he had been thinking seriously at all, it had been reluctantly, as he purposely stretched out the time for healing—before decisions about his life. He had been alone. Now he was less surprised by finding men behind him, intent upon his death, than he was by the fact that he was responsible not only for his own life but for a woman's, and he *cared*. Was he a fool for caring? There was no time to debate it with himself, and perhaps he had debated with himself far too much lately. He knew only that he wanted to get out of this not merely for himself but for her. At this moment, as near death as he had been in a long time, he felt all his feeling intensify. It was as if his body, feeling the danger, wanted to make sure he understood how good life could be. He had to make this and see what was next. Even if it was bleak disappointment, he could handle it. She had helped him want to *live* again.

He was stiffening up even in the moments he had paused. His arm and leg muscles, pressed beyond their endurance, began to tremble. He knew he had to move now or he would not be able to move at all.

Straightening from the slight crouch he was in, he reached upward with his left hand, hanging onto the tuft of thick, tough brush with his right. He felt around with numbed fingertips.

When he first touched it, he thought it was some sort of lichen.

He tried to grasp it.

It moved.

The thing—heavy and furry and moving with terrifying speed —ran over his hand and shot down his arm, across his shoulder. He caught a glimpse of it—fat, long hairy legs, as big as his hand —*tarantula*.

The spider scuttered across his chest and ran up onto his face. The legs pressed with firm lightness against his mouth and nose. The tarantula paused, fibrillating, trying to make some decision. It had a dry odor.

Nothing mattered but getting the damned thing *off* him. Doug dashed at it with his free left hand, feeling legs and furry body in his fingers as he jerked his hand across his forehead, catching it and hurling it convulsively away from him. It went free.

So did his balance.

The convulsion had swung one leg away from the cliff. His weight sagged outward, supported by one foot and his hand clutching the handful of brush growing from between the rocks. He felt the brush begin to tear loose at the roots. He was going to fall. He clawed with his free hand. A chunk of rock broke loose and tumbled—he grabbed again.

His hand caught the jagged edge of a rock. His fingers tightened spasmodically—held—and he swung inward. Rocks gouged his chest. He dug with his toes for a hold, and then the brush that had saved his life came out under his right hand and his hand slid down, fingernails breaking against the rocks, gouging— and held in a crack.

Heart crashing, he lay against the cliff.

Part of him wanted to give up, to stay precisely in this position forever, not move again. The *fall* was part of him now, like the cliff. His belly gusted with panic. Other spiders, he thought. A nest of them just over his head. He couldn't reach again.

Behind him somewhere—very definitely—he heard a distant sound.

They were coming.

Sheer rage—at them, at the cliff, at his fear, at all of it—probably saved him.

Without thought, he reached up again into almost the precise spot where the huge spider had been. There might be more, a nest. If another furry thing moved, he would go up anyway. There was nothing else he could do. He would just *move,* and it didn't matter any more; he had to get this over with, do it or be done.

He grabbed a hold and lunged up, dug in his feet, reached up and caught another hold, swung outward, found a rock, clambered swiftly. The cliff felt him and relaxed and helped, offering a sharp-edged projection to his clawing fingertips. He used it and got a toehold and reached over and felt the heavy earth lip, slightly overhanging. Feeling around, he got hold of an exposed tree root. It held. He grasped it with one hand, then both, and hurled himself upward in a final lunge.

His head topped the edge and he hauled himself up, shoulders, then chest and then stomach, up onto the lip. With one last convulsive effort, his weight hanging for an instant on the shelf of his own ribs, he threw himself up and over, rolling away from the edge.

For a few seconds he lay flat on his back, sobbing for air, staring up at the vault of the stars.

CHAPTER 11

Pressed against the corners of her hiding place, Ruth heard them coming.

She had been motionless, alone, for what seemed a very long time. She had heard the crumbling sounds of rock falling, signaling Doug's ascent of the cliff wall. Now for a long, torturous time it had been silent. So he was up, she thought. But that seemed to make very little difference now. As the sounds of stealthy movements neared, coming along the narrow gully in the blackness from her left, the fear only changed quality from dread to intense near panic.

They made little noise. She could hear their feet crunching gravel. Now and then something brushed against a limb or some weeds. There was nothing else. The shrubs and creepers around her boxlike rock place blocked all vision and she cowered, on her knees with her shoulder against the wall, every nerve tight.

The sounds continued to approach until each pebble noise was distinct, and she could hear them breathing. They were right upon her.

A voice said very softly, "Are you sure?"

Ruth held her breath.

"There's no other way for them," the other voice—Crewser's—replied just as softly.

They were moving directly past her hiding place, less than

five feet away. She heard the crunch of gravel and dirt under their feet, the rustle of their clothing. They were moving steadily, without haste, passing her place.

The first voice, which might have been Buckingham's, muttered, "They could have gone the other way."

"He knows the lay of the land," the other voice replied softly. "This is their only chance and he knows it."

"They didn't climb out?"

"She couldn't."

"Dave will stop them, then."

"Be quiet."

Their voices were very soft. She knew they were so close she could have moved only slightly, reached out and touched them. Her eyes were squeezed shut and her hands, in tight fists, pressed against her chest. Every muscle strained tight, hurting.

"I wish it hadn't come to this. I wish we'd let them go."

"I said be quiet!"

"Yeah, but if they get away now—"

"We can't let them."

"But if they do—"

"They *won't.*"

"But if somehow—"

"*Shut up!*"

The sounds of their bodies moved slightly past her hiding place. She allowed herself a shallow, shuddering breath.

So Doug had been right. She had tricked them, and as she saw how easy it had been, surprise seeped in on her. Why hadn't Doug hidden with her? Then both of them could have doubled back.

The answer came immediately: Without some resolution ahead, the pursuers would quickly turn back. The chase would resume. It was too far from town for any real escape, and the chance of help was even more remote. Doug had seen this: There was no escaping; the only question lay in how the showdown was to come.

Crewser and Buckingham moved on away from her, their sounds fading. Ruth remained very still, remembering what Doug had told her. She had to trust to his plan. Already it had worked better than she had hoped. Crewser and Buckingham had moved right past her, and by now she could faintly hear them as they worked on down the gully, rapidly going away from her. He had understood their tactics; he had fooled them. This was the thing she had to keep in her mind, and trust him. It wouldn't do to imagine what might still happen if he made a mistake—it wouldn't help to think about the odds. She had to do her part as he had ordered.

She forced herself to wait. Finally there was nothing but silence. She opened her eyes and saw the dim walls of the gully, the faint sky.

Then, very carefully, she got to her feet and left her hiding place. She turned and started down the ravine the way they had come.

It wasn't far to the intersection of the other deep gully—not nearly as far as it had seemed coming the other way with Doug. The night was deep and still. Insects clattered at a distance, but near at hand the only sound was the tiny ripple of water.

The new ravine was even narrower than the other. She worked her way into it, supporting her balance with a hand flattened against the rock and earth walls on either side. Weeds choked the muddy ground under her feet and she felt she was making a tremendous racket.

In a few minutes the ravine widened to perhaps fifteen feet, and the floor became sandy, with a little trickle of water down its center. She stayed near the wall on her left, moving slowly, her feet making sucking noises in the deep, wet sand. From beyond her hiding place there was no sound of any kind. Somewhere the fatal game was continuing. Doug was alone against the three of them. If he made a mistake . . .

She refused to think about the results that would follow a mistake. There would not be a mistake. Somehow he would trick them and come back for her. Some way they would get out of this and back to town—to McAlester or someplace safe. It occurred to her that she had never heard of McAlester, Oklahoma, before today. Now it seemed the safest and most desirable haven in the world.

She had never been this tired in her life. With every step, her legs trembled and threatened to collapse, but somehow continued to function. Her head throbbed, and in her mouth was the taste of old pennies. That was fear, she thought; she had read about the coppery taste of fear. It hadn't meant anything to her then because she had not known it from her own experience.

So little of this was part of her previous experience. There was by now an intimacy between her and the mud, the jagged stones that cut at her feet and hands, the itchy-wet texture of leaves. Her senses had awakened swiftly and were learning. She knew now how some leaves were broad, slippery-smooth as if waxed, and others were narrow, with a rough feeling to them like a cat's tongue. Her body was learning, too, the sting of a thorn, the variations in shadows from rock to crevice to brush and sky seen momentarily overhead; the thump of a heart worked too hard, and frightened; the warm-clammy sensation of torn clothing against sweat, but with the whisper of night wind cool on the outside, pasting it to little ridges of muscle that ached and pleaded for rest. The earthen odors of her own body came up to her: mud, oil, sweat, stale perfume, gasoline, brackish water, the green rotting freshness of vegetation. She had lived her life cosmeticized, deodorized, shielded from all this reality, she thought. But her body remembered, and she remembered, recognizing all these things with a memory that was not hers but somehow of the race. The mud inside her shoes, gummy between her nyloned toes, was of no more consequence than the itchy trickle of blood in her tangled hair or the burning pain where she had lost skin on elbows and knees, and the crusting flesh broke each time she moved. She could have been safer here, she thought, naked. She could have moved better, felt better by exposing *all* of herself to the ragged edges and slippery mud and furry-rough edges of green leaves.

The sound of the waterfall was close now. She could not see it yet, but the tinkle of water was immediate. She could hear it falling, then breaking on rocks and splashing. With the walls wider here, she could also make out a few minimum features around her. The walls were pocked with holes that looked like craters, some of them deep. How was she to know which cave he had meant?

As she paused to try to solve the problem, she heard the noise behind her.

It was close and it panicked her—the sound of someone moving.

Without thought, she ran to the nearest hole in the rock. She scrambled in. *Dear God, let it be deep.* The noise was louder, a person or animal thrashing through the brush and crossing the mucky sand. A heavy sound.

She crawled deeper into the hole. The rock ceiling sloped down sharply. Her head bumped into it, sharply, stunning her. She groped ahead with her hands. The walls and ceiling converged to a point—the cave was only four or five feet deep and a dead end.

Cowering, she pressed herself as deep into the hole as she could get, making herself into a ball. She was mindless with panic.

Outside the little opening a bright light flashed. Its beam showed bushes, weeds, the little stream of water bright yellow under the light, the legs of a man and his boots in the reflected rays.

The light flashed past the opening of her hiding place, went on, swept back. She pressed desperately back in her hiding place that had now become a trap, and the light shone on the mouth of the hole again—got brighter—penetrated and touched her legs and then became blinding as the light moved nearer and the shaft of it struck dazzlingly full on her face, into her eyes. She was blinded.

A hand reached in and grasped her arm. She struggled weakly, but it was no use. The man was too strong—he had her—and the light stayed on her as she was pulled down the dirt incline and out of the hole into the night again.

"All right," the man's voice said with curiously gentle satisfaction. "All right, now."

It was Chuck Vachon.

Doug approached the outcropping slowly, crawling through the high grass without a sound. He was approximately thirty feet from the motionless, stumplike figure he knew was Dave Smith. Kneeling with his rifle and facing partly the other way—down into the ravine—Smith was precisely where Doug had imagined he would be.

Movement across the top of the ridges had not been difficult, and Doug had made good time. He had come up the steep hill on hands and knees, wondering what new plan he would try if his guess was wrong. But the guess had not been wrong; Smith was here, waiting to head them off in their flight. His lumpy silhouette was black against the starry sky. Beyond his position, the earth dropped vertically into the ravine. Lightning bugs pulsed their little beacons in the void. Except for a single small scrub oak, the edge of the outcropping was open grass, windswept.

Inching forward, Doug held Smith's profile in such concentration that his eyes ached. He no longer felt tired; that was all behind him now, and every nerve was strung tightly ready. He had to get Smith quickly, and preferably without so much as a shot. That was the idea: to get the rifle from him, brain him with it, and wait for Crewser and Buckingham. The second best was to get the rifle any way he could, short of being killed in the process. There was no third best.

Continuing to move through the deep grass, Doug crawled with the infinite care of his old training. It had been ambush of a different kind then, with heavy equipment and the reassuring weight of an M-16 or heavy attack knife in hand. This time he had nothing.

No matter, he told himself. Every movement brought him nearer Smith. The odds were bad but not impossible.

He could make out the outlines of Smith's face now, partly averted, staring intently into the dark ravine. The rifle looked like a 30.06 deer gun with a leather strap. Smith held the butt on his right hip, his finger through the trigger guard, the barrel pointing at the sky. His jacket was open and the soft night wind moved the zippered edges slightly; there was no other movement of any kind. Smith was not a fool; he had stalked big game and knew how to hold a position to avoid warning the prey.

Doug was in the open now, as deep as he could get into the grass, yet entirely visible if Smith so much as glanced in his direction.

The distance between them was about ten feet.

There was always a time on a stalk, Doug had learned, when some sense not fully understood was likely to make its presence known. The victim's skin would crawl, or he would have that uncanny realization that he was being watched. In training the officer had asked what could be done about this, and someone had suggested the age-old trick of not looking directly at the victim, so he would not "feel the eyes on him." Precisely wrong, the officer had said; if the victim felt he was being observed, he would turn. Nothing on God's earth would prevent it. And if he did begin to turn, it was up to you, the attacker, to have him under such magnifying scrutiny that the first, tiniest trace of movement warned you that the time for stealth was over and the time for attack had come.

Very often, the officer had told them, the first sign of a victim's awareness was a hand absently to the back of his neck, as if the man felt some psychic chill.

Doug was about nine feet from Smith. Smith raised his left hand and brushed the short hairs on the back of his neck. Then, instantly, he began to turn toward Doug's position.

Doug lunged to his feet as the movement started.

Smith's head came on around. Doug had taken two steps. A little surprised sound came from his lips. The rifle barrel came around. His reactions were shockingly quick. Doug's feet drove against the hard earth and he left his feet to dive.

The rifle went off. Orange smoke flashed and something tore into Doug's body like a hot poker. The explosion deafened him. He hit Smith fully in the chest with head and shoulder, bowling him over. His deafness allowed no hint of sound. The rifle flew in the air. Smith shot a knee into Doug's mid-section and Doug fell over him, still stunned by the pain and noise, but then the training took hold and he managed to catch Smith's collar and hurl him sideways by brute force.

Smith fell heavily on his side, scrambling in the eerie silence to get back on his feet. Doug kicked his left leg out from under him. Smith went down again. Leaping, Doug came down atop him with both elbows together into the face. Things broke and red spurted. In a convulsive reaction, Smith stabbed fingers into Doug's eyes and rolled clear, bobbing to his feet.

Doug sprang up to face him.

Smith, blood pouring from his nose and mouth, reached down and scooped up the rifle. He had it by the barrel. He took a step toward Doug and swung it in a wild arc. Doug went underneath it and drove his shoulder into Smith's middle, bending him over. They piled to the ground and Doug's legs swung out over the edge of the cliff. He scrambled to keep his balance—not to fall into the ravine—and Smith was free again, slamming both hands into Doug's face and then descending on him with knees and elbows going.

Doug rolled and covered up. His brain was on fire now, and so was the central section of his body, and he felt the dizzy yellow vertigo that said he was hurt—badly hurt. That first shot.

He watched himself, like a sleepwalker, block Smith's wide-swinging blow and straighten him up with a vicious chop across the throat. Smith dived for the fallen rifle again, grabbed it and came back to his feet. He tried to work the action but it hung up. His face twisted beyond all recognition, he rushed at Doug, the rifle raised like a club over his head.

Doug, his back to the precipice, dropped to one side and kicked at Smith's legs.

Smith's momentum carried him past Doug—over the edge.

For a wild, impossible instant he looked like the cartoon character who runs out onto space, then pumps his running legs so fast that he manages, impossibly, to get back to firm ground. The rifle flew into space, and Smith desperately flailed arms and legs and almost seemed to *hang* in space for the smallest eyelash movement of time.

Then he dropped.

Doug's hearing came back with Smith's despairing scream. Then came a muffled crash, the sliding of rocks, and silence.

Kneeling at the brink, Doug struggled for air. He was dizzy; he looked down at himself and saw the rapidly spreading wetness all over one side of his shirt. The feeling of being wounded was always new, a soft sense of shock and incredulity mixed with the pain, the thought that *It's really me, I'm really hurt,* so much more intimate and frightening than anyone could ever imagine.

With palsied hands he raised his shirt and looked for the wound. Felt for it.

Smith had shot him slightly to the left of center in the midsection, and the slug had torn a very big hole. Blood pulsed from it with every heartbeat.

Very bad, he thought. *Very* bad. He had seen men die like this, from wounds like this. The bullet went in, perhaps sportsmen did not use bullets as cruel as the tumbling, poison-smeared slugs everyone used in Nam. But a hunting bullet was bad enough.

Smith, he thought, had killed him.

With a great effort he got to his feet. The rifle was down below. If he went down some way and got the rifle, he could have a chance. He had to do that.

But then the sky tilted and the earth came up softly to meet him and he was lying on his side, hurting badly. He struggled to one elbow. The pain intensified. An infinite lassitude stole over him in a single wave motion. He lowered himself gently back to the earth.

The earth smelled faintly rotten and green and dusty. Strange —it had rained, yet here the earth and brush were dry. It hadn't rained here. Local storm. Strange. Clouds came and moved in narrow bands, and here the grass pressed against his face was coarse, its tendrils itchy against his mouth and nostrils, faint odor of green dust, and in his body a stealing, creeping warmth with the pain, dimming it.

It seemed very natural and right to be lying in the grass this way, the warmth in his body. Doug thought distantly about the others and about Ruth. They would have heard the shot and would be warned. He had spoiled things. Stupid. Ruth would be hiding. Would they find her? They would find her. Stupid of him. What else could he have done? He didn't know, and the process of trying to re-examine all his actions and motivations was enormously complex and difficult, and he was simply too tired. He lay with his eyes open, staring at the grass and earth and a tiny slice of the starry sky in his peripheral vision. Bleeding.

He felt such sharp regret. There was always so much to do that was postponed and half forgotten. The cataloguing. No one would do the cataloguing now and he hated to leave it unfinished. His car, too: Who would remember his car? He had left a couple of sex novels on the end table in his house; he wished he had thrown them away so someone would not go in and find them and think badly of him. There was so much he should have done. Now there would be none of it. He had thought one day he would go back to Hawaii. The wishing for Hawaii was intense and painful as he recalled everything about the sun-bright surf and feeling of warm air on wet-salty skin.

Wet-salty skin . . . and Ruth. Two days, all the impossible dreams, not formed until this instant, and now seen clearly, as if part of him had known from the outset and had been making all these plans and hopes for her—for the two of them together. But he had refused to recognize the desires until now, when they came clear to him in the pattern of regret.

It was all very mixed up. He was thinking of her and wanting her and hating it that he had let her down, and they would kill her now, and that was unfair, and the earth was dusty in his nostrils and the pain throbbed with a rhythm that he did not recognize at first and then knew was his heart. He could not move. He was beginning to move back into the earth, a part of him seeping into it now, and things did not seem to matter quite so much.

And then there was sound and movement. He saw something again. Movement in front of his face.

Something—someone's hands—reached down and grasped his shoulders and rolled him onto his back.

Through the shimmering crimson curtain of pain caused by the sudden disturbance, he looked up and managed to recognize the faces of the two men looking down at him. Of course he had expected them.

Chuck Vachon drove like a maniac.

Right now, not a light on, he rocketed the Ford sedan down the humpy, twisting gravel road at a speed that kept as many tires in the air as on the ground. Trees, rocks, ditches and embankments flashed past in the dimness. Twisting the wheel hard to the right, then spinning it back to the left, he took a sharp curve on two wheels that cried out and hurled near-invisible clouds of dust and gravel as the sedan went sideways for an instant and then shuddered straight again as he poured more fuel into the carburetors. Everything rattled. Ruth hung onto the edge of the dash.

"You sure it's Two-Tree?" Vachon yelled at her, his eyes intent on the impossible road.

"I don't know the name. Those trees over there—the high bluff."

"Mighty fine, mighty fine," Vachon bellowed. "Makes sense. Best place for spotting stuff. Quicker this way. Hang on, now."

They had vaulted up a steep grade and now bounced onto a level spot where another section-line road, weed-choked and barely recognizable, intersected. Vachon slammed on the brakes, locking the wheels, and went around sideways, feeding gas at the precise instant necessary to catch the slide and make the car bolt onto its new line. Ruth was thrown part way across the seat, caught herself, sat up and hung on again.

She had known, in the moment he dragged her from the cave, that it was over. Vachon, grim under the brim of his Western hat, had had a huge revolver in his hand. His eyes had been bleak.

"Where are they at?" he had asked her softly.

"They're—I don't know," she had lied, shaking her head.

"You better know," he had told her then with an edge in his tone. "They're fixing to kill that long-hair friend of yours."

That was when she had looked up at him with the dawning realization that she had been wrong about him. His eyes, meeting hers, showed dully that he understood this precisely. Even in the darkness she saw the bitterness in him.

"Well?" he grunted.

She had told him in a rush, and he had then dragged her, running, to the field nearby where the Ford was waiting.

Hanging on now, she didn't know exactly what he planned. But there was a fierce elation—a release—in his savage mistreatment of the car. Nothing could happen to him, she felt. Every time before, she had seen him in situations that were alien to him; now, the car banging through the dark, wheels skidding, dirt flying, radio gear under the instrument panel bouncing around, the revolver on the seat beside him and violence in the air, he was in his element. It was not frightening to her just because it was new. Chuck Vachon, or someone like him, was the only kind of person who could handle this, and the insanity of his driving was a part of this personality. Every shattering bump and new swerve was exhilarating in its recklessness. *Faster,* she thought. *Get us there. Go through the fences, across ditches, I don't care.* Yielding was total release.

With a sudden, hard-sawing action on the brakes, Vachon slowed the car and swung the wheel to the right. There was no road. The sedan smashed into and then over a ditch, simply flattened the puny fence wires and posts in the high weeds and plowed out into the field, knocking down head-high trees and brush. The car bounced over hidden rocks, the tires slammed into holes, rolling over side to side like a stricken boat. The ignition was off and they coasted like a runaway train.

Up ahead a few hundred yards she saw the tall bluff Doug had pointed out to her.

Vachon picked up the revolver and a long aluminum flashlight and popped his door open as the Ford's momentum began to die in the high brush. Things scraped and screamed along the underside.

"Stay here," he snapped as the car lurched to a halt.

"No. I want to come."

He glanced at her and paused for an instant. The quiet of night

145

was around them except for bugs and the cracking of the car engine as it began to cool.

"All right," he muttered. "If I say duck, you duck. If I say drop, you drop. Whatever I say, you do."

Ruth nodded and climbed out her side of the car. The brush was waist high.

Not waiting for her, Vachon ran around the car and started across the field toward the bluff at a loping pace unusually graceful for such a heavy man. She staggered after him, losing ground. She wondered why he hadn't driven closer, then understood he could not have driven closer without being overheard. The sound of them racketing down the road must have carried for miles. But a car on the road was not necessarily a threat, even in this isolation. Would the men on the bluff—or wherever they were—be warned?

She fought the brush to run faster but was opening the gap between them. A creeper caught her ankle and she fell heavily. Getting back to her feet, she saw Vachon's bulky shadow well ahead, clambering over some sort of fallen rock formation. He dropped out of sight on the far side and then reappeared, starting up the steep grassy slope of the bluff.

There was no time to think. All her effort went to increasing her own speed. She fell twice more before she reached the rocks. She was impossibly incompetent out here. The thought goaded her to move faster, recklessly.

Vachon was now more than halfway up the hill, and above him was silent darkness. She saw him turn and glance back down on her, then go on, lowered now from the waist, maintaining a reduced profile.

She reached the shattered rocks. A cliff had been exposed to the elements by centuries of wind and rain, and then had collapsed. It formed a long, crumbled wall that ran along the base of the bluff. She attacked it, fell, tried again, struggled up and slid down the far side, tearing flesh from both her elbows. It didn't matter.

All that mattered was getting there. She had heard the shot as they got into Vachon's car—that single, distant, hollow report of a rifle. Vachon had paused just an instant, his head up like a lion's as he listened, seemed positively to sniff the air. He hadn't speculated aloud, nor had she. *One shot.* A single shot for Doug? One of them sighting down the barrel and pressing the trigger slowly and watching him throw his hands up and fall, broken? *One shot.* A single report as Doug got the gun from one of them and turned the others back, so that now he was up there alone, at bay, armed, waiting for the help Vachon represented?

He couldn't have been hurt now, she thought. Not now, with help here. It would be all right. Things didn't turn out badly. Other people had tragedies. She had even had a tragedy of her own. That was her share. *Not Doug,* she thought as she fought to climb faster. *Not again.*

The slope was steeper than she had imagined. It was hard going. Bent well forward, she angrily ignored the searing exhaustion in her legs and kept going, staggering now and then. Up above, Vachon was nowhere to be seen. The thought crossed her mind that they were badly separated and if something went wrong she could be caught by the others. And Doug was *somewhere,* and she was out of it. Gasping for breath, she managed to increase her pace, learning how to lean harder forward as she stepped up. Her feet slid in the loose soil, but she had also learned to keep forward momentum instead of fighting to balance every little trick of movement.

She neared the top. The brush seemed to thin out and then it became dense grass, only a little higher than her ankles. Along this side of the bluff, a few paces ahead, was a slender line of trees, bent silent in the dimness by the force of daytime winds. She realized that Vachon had brought them to the far side of the formation, so that they could approach from the rear. The place Doug had pointed out to her—whence the shot had come?—was on the other side. Not far.

She climbed over a jumble of stones, caught her leg on an old strand of barbed wire in the grass and pulled free with a gasp of pain as the barbs tore the flesh on her ankle. The ground leveled. She limped ahead.

The top

Vaguely aware of the distant rolling night panorama on all sides, she felt the wind pluck coolly at her torn clothing. She had reached the line of small trees, but they were not dense and she saw a wink of white light beyond them, perhaps fifty yards away, on the far side.

She ran toward the light. Thorn branches lashed at her out of the dark.

Breaking out of the trees, she could see ahead. The far edge of the bluff was naked except for a single, stunted tree near the brink. Vachon stood with his back to her, his flashlight in one hand and his revolver in the other. The cone of light spread in the blackness, illuminating two men standing near the precipice, their hands slack at their sides. One, she recognized, was Alvin Crewser.

She ran nearer, halving the distance.

"Not too close!" Vachon called sharply, his back to her.

She stopped and edged nearer step by step. She saw that the man with Crewser was Paul Buckingham, and on the ground were two rifles near their feet, and then—between them and Vachon—she saw the body.

"*Doug!*"

It was as if she had not cried out. No one reacted. Vachon held the revolver leveled. She could not see his face, but she saw Crewser's face, and Buckingham's face, and their eyes with the flashlight beam in them were like bloody glass.

"You don't understand!" Crewser said hoarsely.

Vachon stood motionless. "You did it."

Ruth chilled at the sound of his voice. It had no tone. It was utterly flat, without inflection, deathlike.

And she *knew*. The knowledge plunged into her body like a spiked icicle, filling her. She stood rooted.

Alvin Crewser was a different man again, neither the one she had known in town nor the one of the tunnel. He was stripped of everything but his desperation. "Do you think we *wanted* it?" he asked.

"No," Vachon said wearily. "I don't suppose you did."

Buckingham, standing beside Crewser, said nothing. He trembled as if he were in a trance. Saliva gleamed wetly on his chin, drooling from his slack mouth. He was petrified.

"They were going to *kill* him," Crewser choked. "Press just wanted to stop them. That's all we intended to do. Then we went there and they killed Press and it was too late. Don't you see that, Chuck?"

"All these years," Vachon said. "You hid this."

"We would have gone to *prison*. Everybody would have thought Noble was a—was a bad place."

"You killed them," Vachon said. He sounded horribly like a robot, a machine without feeling, a thing programmed to act blindly.

"You don't know how we wished it was different," Crewser said passionately. "My God, and then when that other man came, and we had to do something about *him*—"

"But you kept right on."

"We tried to make her go away! We lied, and then we tried to give her enough information so she would leave. But then when she found the old woman, we knew it was too late again. We didn't want it to happen! Do you understand that? We *hated* it! We—"

Slowly, Vachon's leonine head rolled from side to side. "You just kept right on. You kept on lying and breaking the law. You treated me like a friend. You kept right on killing."

"Once it started, we couldn't get *out*," Crewser said, and suddenly his thin composure broke, and he sobbed. "We wanted to get out, Chuck."

"Ah," Vachon said softly, with a gentle, bitter regret. "God damn you, Al. You lied to all of us. You *killed,* and you *lied.*"

Buckingham stood trembling, drooling spittle like an idiot fascinated by a candle. Crewser, tears gleaming on his cheeks, held out his hands—shockingly small, feminine hands—in supplication. Watching, rooted in her horror, Ruth understood totally. It was so clear that anyone could have seen. Crewser's doom was written in every line of Vachon's stance, in every nuance of his whispered condemnation.

But Crewser did not quite yet see.

"Anybody would have done the same," he wept. "Anybody! After it started, what else could we do? Do you think I liked it? Do you think—can you imagine how I felt? *I* had to be the leader! *I* had to make the decisions! I'm not smart or a leader, but they *made* me act that way, and it was all up to me—somebody had to do it! I'm just an ordinary man—"

"Ah," Vachon breathed again. "God damn you to hell, Al."

Finally, Crewser saw.

"Chuck!" he screamed. "*Listen* to me!"

Vachon's body shook as if rocked by orgasm. The revolver exploded. Crewser was blown backward by the impact of the bullet. His face was shocked, hurt, childlike in its inability to understand.

He went off the cliff and fell.

From somewhere below came a hideous smashing sound, then a rumbling of falling rocks and heavy things and gravel—and silence.

Vachon swung the revolver fractionally toward Buckingham. The chubby figure moaned and dropped to its knees, holding out its hands in supplication. "No, Chuck! *No!* My God!"

Vachon spoke. "Pick up the rifles."

Stunned, Ruth managed to understand he was speaking to her. On wooden legs she stumbled forward and picked up the two heavy firearms. Buckingham, very near her, was sobbing, mouthing incoherent words. She smelled his terror, like the spoor of a wounded animal. She forced herself to look at Doug on the ground and saw the blood everywhere. A moan broke from her.

"Get them guns to the car," Vachon said. "You," he added to Buckingham. "Help me carry him."

Buckingham nodded and swayed to his feet, pathetically eager, seeing a way to escape death. His face in the beam of Vachon's flashlight glistened with tears and mucous.

Vachon grabbed Ruth's arm and spun her. "You think I didn't have to."

"No. I—"

"I know what you think. I don't give a God damn what you think."

The flashlight suddenly went out, and she was almost blind. But she saw Vachon hold up a fist toward the cowering Buckingham. Vachon shook from head to foot.

"Eleven years. Eleven goddamned *years!*"

Ruth thought he was going to kill Buckingham too. She understood on some level below words that he would kill Buckingham, too, because he must.

Buckingham, kneeling beside Doug, looked up. He did not move or make a sound. For the first time, locked in this instant with Vachon, he seemed to understand. His face changed. He accepted it, and—funny little man with bushy hair growing out to be mod—he did not cower.

The wind moved. Ruth saw Buckingham's eyes, and the truth opened up for her, and she knew as he did—she *knew.*

Vachon dropped the revolver to his side. His shoulders slumped.

"C'mon," he muttered and bent to help Buckingham lift Doug's body.

Ruth shudderingly breathed.

It was over. They were people again.

CHAPTER
12

The emergency room in the McAlester hospital was small, very brightly lighted and very crowded. There had been an automobile accident and two teen-age boys lay unconscious on wheeled carts in the hall. Another boy was behind one of the treatment-room doors. A young doctor and two nurses had a small child—victim of some other blind chance—in the other room and were administering oxygen. In the tiny, yellow-walled alcove off the hall, Ruth sat in a straight plastic chair and pulled on her cigarette and tried to come the rest of the way back to the world. They stood and sat all around her.

"I'm not sure I have it all straight," the youthful district attorney said. He was painfully slender and had come from bed; he wore baggy summer slacks and a tee shirt and needed a shave. His assistant, an older man with the odor of defeat around him, stood beside him taking notes. "They were trying to kill you," the district attorney said.

Vachon, a hulk in the chair beside her, unfolded massive hands and spread them on his lap. "I'll have a full report."

The sheriff was there too. A tiny man with no hair on his head, he stood at the corner of the alcove, hatless, wearing a calico shirt and Levis and boots, with a womanlike little gun, pearl-handled, in a flowery leather holster on his belt.

"The boys are probably there by now," he said. "Collecting the bodies."

"You told them about Spandecker," Vachon half questioned. "In the mine tunnel."

"Right," the sheriff said. He was being brisk and efficient.

Vachon took a deep breath. "I found him first."

"Let's just recap this," the district attorney suggested, trying to maintain some sort of order that his grim expression betrayed he needed badly. "You knew they were after these two people. You had them under surveillance—"

"I watched," Vachon grunted. "I seen what Smith did to the long-hair's car. You've already got that."

The district attorney scowled. "Yes. Right. And then today—"

"Luck," Vachon said stolidly.

"When they had disappeared, you returned to keep a watch on, uh . . ." The young lawyer paused and snapped his fingers.

"Crewser," the older assistant supplied from the notes.

"Crewser," the district attorney said as if his aide didn't exist.

Vachon sat round-shouldered, a docile bull allowing them this.

A doctor came out of one of the rooms beyond the treatment area, gestured to the sheriff and had a brief whispered conversation with him in the hall. The sheriff nodded and came back.

"The long-hair's in surgery," he said.

"He has a name," Ruth snapped.

The sheriff's eyebrows went up. "Huh?" His intonation made her think, irrationally, of Lum and Abner.

"Doug," she spat at him. "Doug Bennett. That's his *name*. Use it "

The sheriff sighed, gave the district attorney a look that said she was hysterical and leaned against the wall again.

The district attorney said, "You found Spandecker and then followed the others. Is that right?"

Vachon kept his head down. "That's right," he said, submitting to the stupidity of it.

"The victim, uh—"

"Bennett."

"Bennett evidently killed, uh—"

"Smith."

"The victim Bennett evidently killed Smith, one of the men chasing him and Miss Baxter here—"

"Mrs. Baxter."

"—but he was shot, and that was when you located Mrs. Baxter, here, and intervened."

The district attorney paused. No one said anything. Ruth looked down at her bloodstained arms and legs, the shreds of her clothing. She was numb. The cigarette was down to the filter and had gone out. It remained between her fingers.

"Is that correct?" the district attorney pressed.

"You got it right," Vachon grunted.

"I find the other part," the district attorney said, "rather hard to believe."

Vachon roused himself. "Do you, now? Well, I swan."

The lawyer's face colored under the sarcasm. "You say it's your understanding these men killed some other men eleven years ago?"

Vachon took a deep breath and straightened, addressing himself wearily to the routine. "You got Buckingham. He'll give it all."

"Suppose you reiterate your understanding."

God. They were so stupid. They plodded along. Vachon began telling it again, but Ruth did not listen, allowing his voice to drone into oblivion. She already knew it, as much as anyone knew, from the talk in the car on the way.

Buckingham had told them. He had wept as he told it, as if glad after all this time to have it out of him, even if the sharing meant his doom.

Press Bartelson and the others had been members of the Sportsmen's Club. So had Gerald Spandecker, Leo Huffman and Frank Tubbs. Huffman, Buckingham said, had been the instigator. He had been the one who convinced Spandecker and Tubbs that the President of the United States had to be killed when he came to Archer County to dedicate the road.

The others had not known of this until Press Bartelson had stumbled into their planning session in the old barn the night before the road ceremonies. Huffman, Spandecker and Tubbs were committed by then, and their insanity made a strange kind of sense to them. They had new, high-powered rifles, bought by Huffman in Kansas City, fitted with telescopic sights in Tulsa. They would be in the woods, at three locations already chosen with great care on ostensible hunting trips.

When the President cut the ribbon—at that precise instant—they would all fire.

Press, having come upon their plan, had been given the opportunity to join them. He had refused and had gone back to Noble. He was the club president, the hero of the town, their friend. Somehow it never occurred to them that he would tell anyone or try to intervene.

Press had gone to Crewser, Buckingham, Smith and another member named Adam Frings and told them what was taking place. Press said the would-be killers had to be stopped. He said the three men would give it up if the rest of them went back to the barn immediately and told them it was insane, it couldn't be allowed, it would be stopped by force if necessary.

We're all friends, he had told them. We can stop it. We don't need to have anybody arrested or have any bad publicity for the town. When Jerry and Leo and Frank see how set against them we are, they'll give it up. They're just excited—Leo is practically out of his head on this issue—and we can make them give it up.

So they had driven into the country, the four of them, taking their own rifles to prove to their friends they meant business.

They went into the barn. Press started talking. Leo Huffman went berserk, grabbed his rifle and fired. Press went down. Crewser, Buckingham, Smith and Frings fired at their friends in instant frightened retaliation.

Afterward it had been worse. Press was dying, shot in the lungs and clearly beyond help. Huffman was dead; Spandecker was dead; Tubbs lay dying. Then, in the shocked aftermath, it had been Crewser who said no one would ever believe it, no one would ever understand, the town would never get over this kind of blow.

It had to be hidden.

Buckingham and Smith had taken the bodies of Huffman, Spandecker and Tubbs in the Spandecker car, driven it to the high cliff, drenched the insides with gasoline, set a match to it and let it roll and plunge down into the gorge where it scattered and burned intensely.

Crewser and Frings took Press toward town. He had no chance to live. They took him into the country and rigged the hunting-accident story, letting someone else find him the following day. He was found still alive, and for days he clung to the shreds of his life while they wondered if he could have been surely saved if they had not given up on him. And then finally he had died after all.

Later, Buckingham had told them in the car, someone had come to Noble, looking for Spandecker. Dave Smith had been the one who insisted the stranger had to be stopped, and it had been Smith and Frings who killed him, a man named Concannon.

Frings had never been able to live with that. He had moved away. He lived now, Buckingham thought, in the Los Angeles area.

"Why did the kid get in it?" the district attorney was asking now. "The one that the mine roof fell on. Ted Spandecker," he said quickly, while his assistant shuffled note pages looking for the name. "He was one of the victims' sons, right?"

Vachon nodded. "Right."

"Why would *he* help the men who had killed his father?"

Ruth remembered Ted Spandecker in the tunnel. "He didn't want it known," she said.

"What?"

She looked at the lawyer. He was so young and intense. All the intense young men, she thought, and felt very old. "He didn't want it known," she repeated.

"I don't understand that."

A city policeman hurried down the corridor. "They're back in the car over there," he said. "They're reporting in. You can listen to it on the radio in the car outside, if you want."

The sheriff nodded. "I want to hear that."

"I do too," the district attorney said. He looked at Ruth. "We'll want to talk more." He turned to his aide. "Coming?"

They trooped out, leaving Ruth and Vachon alone in the alcove. They said nothing. Over their heads, a hospital signal bell made its demanding clicking sound. Vachon sat with his hands folded, very still. Failure, she thought, understanding. Problem drinker. Stupid, crude, wasted, narrow, embittered man, measuring out the dregs from a life that was never more than an echo of a dream, awaiting these moments when something can make sense, and then be gone again.

"You aim to tell them?" he asked finally, not looking at her.

"No," she said.

"You ain't?" He was surprised but quiet.

"No," she repeated and felt almost a fondness for him in this moment when she understood and could give this to him. He had been given so little.

His big hands folded and unfolded in his lap, powerful hands with scars, yet childish. "Thank you," he said.

She felt the tears come. She did not reply. It was not the way she wanted it and he was not—but then she was not, either. This feeling in her now, she thought, was reality.

One of the young doctors walked briskly down the hall and smiled at her. "Let's take a look at you now, shall we?"

She got to her feet and followed him. They went into one of the treatment rooms. It had shiny metal equipment and sterile shelves and a long plastic table that was high, and a nurse stood there watching her.

The doctor patted the table. "Up here, please. Can you make it?"

She could make it. The plastic was still warm from the last person. It was an assembly line. But that didn't matter either.

The nurse turned on the bright dish light overhead. It shone into her eyes like Vachon's flashlight, magnified. The doctor's cool, efficient hands began touching cuts and scratches on her face and head. "Does that hurt?"

"Will he live?" she asked in reply.

The doctor looked at the nurse. His forehead wrinkled. "I don't know," he said. "We can certainly hope so, can't we?"